'What the hell's the meaning of this?'

'I want an explanation.' Nathan's lean forefinger stabbed at the newspaper. The caption below the photo announced that it was of Dr Rowan Stewart and her new toy-boy secretary, Matthew Pride.

'Pride,' Rowan croaked through parched lips. 'Matthew Pride.'

'My son.'

'I didn't know whose son he was. Does it matter?'

'I will not be made a figure of fun. Matthew isn't working for you any longer.'

'We'll see about that!'

Dear Reader

We introduce Abigail Gordon this month, with her first book JOEL'S WAY, in which Bethany finally learns how she and Joel were parted in the past. Flora Sinclair's second book, PRIDE'S FALL, has Nathan's son Matthew trying to be matchmaker, with unforeseen hassles! And we meet Zena Winters again, first seen in MORE THAN MEMORIES by Judith Worthy; are her problems with Gavin insurmountable in ONLY THE LONELY? And finally, an absolutely delightful heroine in student nurse Phoebe James, who captivates Magnus—but is he too old for her? Enjoy!!

The Editor

Flora Sinclair was born in and grew up outside London. She went north to study psychology at university but returned to work in a London hospital. She now lives in Scotland, dividing her time between Glasgow and a remote Hebridian island.

Recent titles by the same author:

DOCTOR ALONE

PRIDE'S FALL

BY

FLORA SINCLAIR

MILLS & BOON LIMITED
ETON HOUSE   18–24 PARADISE ROAD
RICHMOND   SURREY   TW9 1SR

All the characters in this book have no existence outside the imagination of the Author, and have no relation whatsoever to anyone bearing the same name or names. They are not even distantly inspired by any individual known or unknown to the Author, and all the incidents are pure invention.

All Rights Reserved. The text of this publication or any part thereof may not be reproduced or transmitted in any form or by any means, electronic or mechanical, including photocopying, recording, storage in an information retrieval system, or otherwise, without the written permission of the publisher.

This book is sold subject to the condition that it shall not, by way of trade or otherwise, be lent, resold, hired out or otherwise circulated without the prior consent of the publisher in any form of binding or cover other than that in which it is published and without a similar condition including this condition being imposed on the subsequent purchaser.

First published in Great Britain 1993 by Mills & Boon Limited

© Flora Sinclair 1993

*Australian copyright 1993
Philippine copyright 1993
This edition 1993*

ISBN 0 263 78129 1

*Set in 10 on 11½ pt Linotron Times
03-9305-53781*

*Typeset in Great Britain by Centracet, Cambridge
Made and printed in Great Britain*

CHAPTER ONE

WARM brown eyes met, and held, cold grey ones. The gaze lengthened, the silence strained, then brown eyes spoke.

'Don't you think that's a sexist attitude?'

Lashes briefly veiled grey eyes, but raised to reveal a gaze as steady as before. 'Possibly.' There was as little warmth in the voice as in the eyes.

'Isn't that rather. . .dangerous?' There was no threat in the voice, just innocent enquiry. Why, then. . .? Grey eyes lowered lashes again, consulting papers on the desk.

'You realise this is a temporary job, for two months?'

'Yes. That suits me fine, because I'll be starting as a medical student in October.'

'Hmm.' Grey eyes flicked over the c.v. again. 'I still find it strange that you should want this job.'

'I thought I should work over the summer and——'

'There are other jobs, more *suitable*,' the word was emphasised, 'for someone of your. . .' The sentence wasn't completed, as though the speaker realised deep water lay ahead. 'Why *this* job?'

Brown eyes sighed, sounding as though wondering how honest to be. Grey eyes noticed.

'The truth.'

'To be honest, then, I hadn't intended to work this summer, but my father insisted, and——'

'And taking an unsuitable job is your way of getting your own back.'

Brown eyes blushed fiery red. 'You make it sound dubious. There's not a lot of choice; temporary work is hard to find. It's a perfectly respectable job.'

Grey eyes suddenly smiled, transforming the face they inhabited. 'True. But somehow an eighteen-year-old male school-leaver isn't most people's idea of a temporary secretary.'

'I can type perfectly well.' Matthew Laurie sounded affronted that she should be doubting his skills. 'I'm completely capable of using a computer and word processor. We had to learn at school.' He grinned engagingly.

'That's all very well——' Rowan Stewart tried to hold on to her dignity when what she really wanted to do was grin back '—but if you don't really want to work, and you're only interested in this as a way of getting back at your father...well, it doesn't sound much of a recommendation, does it?' Put like that it sounded awful, so why was she even still considering such a stupid idea as employing this engaging young lad?

'I agree it doesn't sound good, but...' He stopped and met her gaze again, holding it steady. 'I promise I'll work hard. I'll do whatever you want.'

'You'll get bored.' She was weakening and they both knew it.

'No, I won't. Not in two months. It will be completely different from anything else I've done.'

You can say that again, Rowan thought, just managing to stop the words tumbling out.

'I can do all sorts of things. And since I'm going into medicine I thought I might learn something useful.'

'And you might not! I need someone to type, run errands, sort things out, possibly do some coding—a "Girl Friday" rather than a research assistant.'

'Man Friday.'

'All right — Man Friday.'

'Then I've got the job?'

'I must be crazy, but. . .yes, you've got the job. A week's trial, at least,' she amended hastily.

'Great!' Matthew seemed genuinely pleased, his warm brown eyes regarding her with an expression that made him look like an eager puppy. With soft brown curly hair flopping over his forehead and lightly tanned skin the description seemed appropriate. 'When do I start?'

'How soon can you?'

'Today.'

'Today?' Rowan was startled.

'If you like.'

She smiled again, and the grey eyes which had clouded over at the rashness of her decision brightened. 'Wonderful. Things are really fraught at the moment. Now we need to get you sorted out at the finance office and Personnel.'

'I can do all that if you just let them know you've employed me.' His voice sounded slightly strained, a frown creeping between his brows, but Rowan was too busy to notice.

'Now part of your salary comes from a grant and part from other sources. Finance knows all about it, and——' Rowan was writing as she spoke.

'I'll handle it.'

'Good. Take this over to their offices on the main campus and then come back here. You'll be working in the room next door. I've got to go to a meeting now, but you can familiarise yourself with the computer and things. . .'

'You go. I'll sort myself out. When will you be back?'

'Lunchtime. Now, the phone——'

'I'll take messages,' Matthew told her. 'Now you go to your meeting. I can manage. Honestly.'

Rowan believed him. He might be young, and male, but he was very bright, judging by his school record, and he sounded competent and in control. . . As she rushed out of the door Rowan reflected that it was too late anyway. Curiosity had made her interview him, but she hadn't intended to give him the job—even though there weren't many people interested in it. She grinned inwardly—it would certainly raise one or two eyebrows in the department. But then didn't she enjoy that?

The meeting was not going well. Rowan needed permission from the division of psychiatry to begin her latest research project. Dr Munro was always difficult. No longer engaged in anything remotely connected with research, he seemed to resent others doing it. He was gradually being won round by others, though, as most of the consultants were in favour of her idea. If only Dr Pride would openly support the project. This was only the third time she had seen him. At first wary of him, having heard his reputation for years before she saw him, she had come to respect him, even though the wariness still remained. Whatever else he was, and there were rumours aplenty, he was essentially a fair man, at least where his work was concerned. If he opposed her programme Rowan knew she wouldn't stand a chance of getting the division's support for it.

She was running out of arguments. And out of time. The consultants were beginning to look at their watches. If she didn't win Dr Munro round soon she never would.

'What's the matter, Henry?' Nathan Pride's voice was as rich and dark and velvety as his eyes.

It was like the cavalry appearing over the crest of the hill, and Rowan gave an imperceptible sigh of relief. If Dr Pride was going to give the project his support there would be no opposition. What would he expect in return? Rowan was not so naïve as to believe that his support would come totally free of strings.

'Dr Stewart's plan is straightforward enough — support groups for patients with schizophrenia. The idea of educating them about the illness seems remarkably sound to me. I can't think why it hasn't been done before. *And* she has the research grant.'

'That's all very well,' Henry Munro muttered, 'but — '

'If you remember, the division's support was given, in principle, before Dr Stewart submitted her grant proposal. This meeting is really formalising and implementing that decision,' Dr Pride cut through his colleague's murmurings, bringing several nods of approval from round the table. Henry Munro was keeping them from their lunch. They trusted Rowan Stewart, for all that she was a psychologist and a woman and only thirty. 'Sound' was how Nathan Pride had described her research, and that was how they thought of her.

'That's settled, then.' Jim Graham brought the meeting to order before Henry could find any more problems, and winked covertly at Rowan, both in support of her project and letting her know that no one had missed who had championed her.

The wink, intercepted by Nathan Pride, caused him to turn his unflinching gaze on Rowan, a slight frown marring his features. For the first time Rowan found herself gazing directly into dark brown eyes, eyes the colour of the peaty water found in her Highland home. Eyes that held the same dark secrets as those deep pools. Eyes which held hers steady. His lashes were ridiculously long for a man, she thought irrelevantly, as her breath caught in her throat. He really did have astonishing eyes. And the rest of him wasn't too bad either, she admitted, having the sensation that she had never looked at him properly before.

His dramatically arched brow lifted and she realised he was aware of her scrutiny. She willed herself not to blush, composing her features into what she hoped was an expression suitable for a competent academic.

'Dr Stewart, a word, please.' His voice cut across the babble of his colleagues as they filed out of the meeting.

Rowan waited for him, wondering what he wanted, and they fell into step along the corridor, her long legs easily keeping pace with his. How come she had never noticed how tall he was before? He topped her own not inconsiderable height by several inches. Or how the breadth of his shoulders owed nothing to his expensive tailoring?

'Do you have time for lunch?'

An immediate longing to say yes was superseded by the memory of Matthew abandoned in her office doing heaven knew what. And then the invitation had been offered in a voice which clearly did not expect to receive a refusal. Nathan Pride had an air about him of getting exactly what he wanted, when he wanted it. Arrogant men were always a challenge to Rowan, and she enjoyed entering battle with them, piercing their arrogance.

Lifting her head slightly, she looked straight at him, ready to decline the invitation, and found that looking into his eyes was like being wrapped in soft, warm velvet, its silken smoothness sliding sensuously over her skin. Pulling her scattered thoughts together, Rowan broke the eye contact and straight away found thinking easier.

'Sorry, I have to get back.' Only slightly breathless, she accompanied the words with her most beguiling smile. It was disconcerting to notice that it didn't have the same effect on Nathan Pride as it did on most men. He merely took it as his due, which did nothing to improve her impression of him.

'I wanted a word with you about my research,' he told her smoothly, not missing a beat and acting as though the invitation had never been made or refused. 'There's something you might be able to help me with.' His lop-sided smile, all practised charm, didn't reach his eyes, which, Rowan noticed, for all their apparent warmth, had a steely depth to them.

This, then, was pay-off time! She hadn't expected it to come so quickly. Admitting to herself that she did owe him something, she made some rapid calculations.

'I could come back late this afternoon, if that's any help to you,' she offered.

His brows creased briefly in concentration, then cleared as he affirmed, 'That will be fine. About four o'clock. My office.' Without waiting for further agreement from her he strode off down the corridor, leaving Rowan wondering just what would be expected of her in return for his unasked-for support.

'Coffee?' Matthew stood at the connecting door, clearly doing his impersonation of the perfect secretary.

'Yes, please.' He might look a bit incongruous, but just now Rowan didn't care. 'Make yourself one and come and join me.'

'How do you take it?' Matthew was already pouring boiling water into two mugs.

'Black, no sugar,' Rowan replied automatically, her eyes widening as she watched him add three heaped spoonfuls of sugar to his own milky drink.

Catching her eye, he grinned. 'I'm a growing lad,' he pointed out reasonably.

'With rotten teeth, if you're not careful.'

Matthew put the coffee in front of her and sat opposite across the desk. Without giving her time to say anything more he picked up a notepad, consulted it briefly and launched into an account of his morning. 'Everything's taken care of with Personnel and Finance. They'll send over something they want you to sign.' He ticked that off his list. 'Here's a list of people who've phoned. I've told them all to phone back between two and three—your diary's empty then,' he added, 'apart from a couple who sounded important, so I'd said you'd ring them. Professor Scott came in and wanted to see you, so I've made an appointment for you with him at three.' He stopped and glanced at her thunderstruck expression. 'It seemed politic,' he explained, 'him being the head of the department and all. I introduced myself. He seemed a bit surprised.'

'I bet.' Rowan shook her head, totally dazed. 'I'll have to introduce you to him properly.'

'Mmm.' Matthew was consulting his list again. 'A Dr MacDonald phoned. I said I was your secretary, and she just laughed and laughed until eventually she hung up. I think she said something about seeing you later.'

Rowan grimaced. She could just imagine her friend's reaction...and the teasing that would be coming her way.

'I think I've got the hang of the computer,' Matthew went on. 'The word-processing package isn't one I'm familiar with, but it looks straightforward enough.' He stopped and smiled at her, so obviously waiting for a pat of approval on the head that Rowan's hand instinctively moved towards him before she checked herself. She really must stop thinking of him as a puppy.

'I'm very impressed', she told him. 'Is your mother a secretary, by any chance?'

It was as though a light inside him was switched off. Suddenly his face was shuttered and he looked years older. 'No, my mother doesn't *work*.' The derision was unmistakable.

'Then how. . .?' She tailed off, realising she should change the subject.

But Matthew's face lightened and he grinned, producing a battered-looking book. 'When you called me for interview I got this book about being a perfect secretary out of the library. I've had it propped in front of me all morning.'

Rowan laughed, relaxing completely for the first time that day. 'Matthew, that's wonderful.' She picked it up and eyed it dubiously. 'It looks a bit dated,' she muttered, flicking through the pages.

Matthew almost snatched it back from her, holding it protectively to his chest. 'That's what's so great about it. Miss — she has to be Miss — Parkinson has very straightforward ideas about secretaries. Clearly defined roles, submissive, courteous, the boss is there to be obeyed and protected——'

'I can't stand it,' Rowan laughingly stopped him, holding up her hands in mock surrender. 'Come on, since it's your first day I'll take you to lunch.'

'Oh, Dr Stewart,' Matthew simpered, 'I'm sure Miss

Parkinson doesn't approve of secretaries lunching with their bosses. In fact, she disapproves——'

'Come on, before I decide hiring you was a very bad idea.' Rowan was still laughing.

'Well, I'm not sure that I should.' Matthew was struggling to keep a straight face.

'I thought the spaghetti place along the road.'

An eighteen-year-old's appetite won out over game-playing. He was across the room holding the door open before she could move. 'After you, Doctor, ma'am.'

Why did it feel like stepping into a spider's web? The door closed behind her and, facing Nathan Pride, Rowan hastily amended her mental picture. A lion's den would be more appropriate. For all his slicked-back hair and dark grey suiting Nathan Pride looked as though he was a close relative of a big cat that stalked its prey with quiet stealth and deadly intent. He smiled, showing even white teeth, and the carnivorous metaphor intensified. Rowan shivered as she imagined those teeth biting into her flesh.

Sinking into a chair, she silently berated herself. She wasn't usually given to such fanciful imaginings over any man, so why this sudden departure from the norm? Crossing long, slim legs, she was aware of Nathan's eyes lingering on them and had to resist the impulse to pull her skirt down. There was nothing wrong with the way she was dressed, and the black skirt of her linen suit sat decorously at her knees. Nevertheless, she tucked her legs under her chair and waited to hear what Nathan Pride would demand of her.

'You may know of the genetics research I'm engaged in,' he said, in the voice of one who would be very surprised to have received a negative reply. 'I think maybe you can be of some help.'

He outlined, clearly and concisely, exactly what he wanted of her. There was nothing as overt as any mention that she might owe him a favour, but it remained there, an unspoken undercurrent. In the event, Rowan was surprised by how little he was asking for. Just for her to enquire of all patients she was going to interview a few simple questions to elicit who might have schizophrenia running through their families. She had a case register set up of several hundred patients, all of whom were to be interviewed by her and her research assistant, so to add a couple of extra questions was no real effort at all. She was surprised when Dr Pride intimated that she might get her name on a paper for her help. She hadn't expected him to be so generous. But it would mean she would still owe him a favour.

As they walked down the for once deserted corridor towards the exit, Rowan was aware of a *frisson* of anticipation. Nathan Pride was being more charming than he need, his arrogance masked by easy familiarity. Would he invite her out for a drink? It was the kind of situation where it would seem quite natural — particularly if she had happened to be a male colleague. Dropping in for a drink was a common occurence. Did being female make such a difference?

What would his wife say? What would *you* say if you were his wife? Rowan asked herself, and was jolted by the realisation that it would be very easy to be jealous of a man like Nathan Pride. It was all too simple to imagine women flinging themselves at his well shod feet, not caring if they were trampled on if it meant he would acknowledge their existence for a while.

They rounded the corner, straight into Anna

MacDonald and her registrar, Mike Knight, who was the only person in the entire hospital who could dwarf Nathan Pride.

'Just the person!' Anna exclaimed, grabbing hold of Rowan before doing a double-take as she finally noticed who her friend's companion was. 'Evening, Nathan.' Her bright smile was only slightly forced as she greeted her colleague. 'Sorry, were you two off somewhere?' She let go of Rowan's arm and looked archly at the other two. Mike Knight merely nodded his head, mumbling a greeting, and did his best to hide a knowing smirk.

Nathan Pride looked slightly startled at the conjecture that was being put on the encounter, and more than a little annoyed as he regarded Rowan with a cold stare of mild distaste.

'Not at all,' he replied smoothly, his voice taking on an arctic quality. 'We'd finished our discussion.' With a curt goodnight which encompassed all three he left them, long legs taking him quickly out of their sight.

'What are you doing with him?' Anna sounded incredulous, and it was only as Mike grinned that they both realised the rest of the conversation might be better conducted in private.

'Bye, Mike,' the women chorused, and he slouched off, his face telling them he knew when he was being deliberately excluded from a good gossip.

'Well?' demanded Anna, wanting an answer to her question. 'You were looking very matey.'

'Mmm.' Rowan eyed her friend dubiously. 'And what, *exactly*, does that mean?'

'His lordship was looking more human than usual. Very pally, in fact. What were you two doing together, anyway? I didn't know you knew him.'

'I don't.' And probably won't, Rowan thought with

something like disappointment. 'He merely wanted a chat after this morning's meeting.'

'Ah!'

'Ah, nothing.' As briefly as she could Rowan outlined the details for Anna. They were in this research project together and she owed it to the other woman to keep her up to date with developments which affected it.

'Sorry if I broke anything up.' Anna sounded more teasing than regretful, and Rowan laughed, knowing it was the expected response.

'Nothing to break up,' she asserted, then wondered why that should be so demoralising.

'Good. I don't trust him an inch.' Anna was unusually negative about this particular colleague. 'Anyway, he never plays around with anyone connected with work.'

'Plays around?' Rowan sounded mildly scandalised. She would have thought Nathan would be very protective of his reputation. Nor did he seem the type to two-time his wife.

'He has a succession of very glamorous girlfriends, but none of them seem to last long. And never anyone in medicine.'

'He's not married, then?' Doing her best to sound casual and uninterested, Rowan was almost holding her breath.

Anna shrugged. 'Unmarried, divorced, I don't know. But forget about him—I'm forgetting the most important thing!' she exclaimed. 'Tell me *all* about your new secretary. Your new *male* secretary.'

Rowan laughed, her good humour restored. 'He's eighteen——'

'Eighteen? Rowan, how could you?'

'Waiting to go to medical school——'

'A baby yet!'

'Very efficient, by the look of things, and——'

'Is he attractive?'

'Yes.'

'I knew it!'

'If you like affectionate puppies,' Rowan added.

'Who doesn't?' Anna laughed. 'When do I get to meet him?'

'Anna, you're incorrigible!'

'Who me?' Anna contrived to sound the injured party. 'You're the one who's employing him!'

There didn't seem to be any answer to that, and once again Rowan hoped she hadn't made a big mistake employing Matthew.

But as she drove home it wasn't Matthew who filled her thoughts, but the difference a genuine smile made to the arrogant but oh, so charming Dr Pride.

Two days later Rowan wondered how she had ever managed without Matthew. Although the job was obviously a game to him, and half the time he seemed determined to play it like a 1960s Doris Day film, nevertheless he was bright, cheerful, efficient and getting through much more work than she had any reason to hope for. Leaning back in her chair, Rowan closed her eyes.

'You work too hard,' said Matthew.

She came upright with a start, her eyes flying wide open. 'I thought you'd gone home.'

'I forgot something.' He looked at her seriously, his grave expression sitting oddly on his young face. 'I mean it.'

'How do you know? You've only been here a couple of days.'

'I've seen the work you take home—and that comes

back finished the next day. I've seen your packed diary, evenings and weekends as well.'

'An academic's life is a tough one!' Rowan tried to laugh as she said it, but somehow her voice broke on the words and it came out sounding more bitter than she had intended.

'And now you're off to this meeting when you'd be better off going home and relaxing.'

'I'm supposed to be the one giving the orders,' she pointed out, but it was obvious to both of them that her heart wasn't in it. 'Anyway, it's not as bad as it looks.' She grinned at him. 'It might sound like a meeting, but tonight it's actually a glorified publicity stunt. A few drinks to which the Press have been invited to try to get them interested in the opening of the new psychiatric research centre and write it up in a sensible and supportive way.' She didn't mention that there was a sneaking hope, lurking at the back of her mind, that Nathan Pride might be there.

'It's still work,' Matthew pointed out with the tenacity of the young.

'True, but I have to go. The people organising it want as many there as possible.' She sighed and stretched. 'You're right, though, it *is* work, and it won't be much fun. I can't even have a drink as I'll have to drive home.'

'I'll drive you.' The offer was made quickly, and surprised Rowan.

'I can't let you,' she protested.

'Why not? I've got my licence. I'm insured. I'll be very careful.'

Rowan was too tired to argue and had already learnt that if Matthew was like a puppy in many endearing ways he also had the characteristic of hanging on to something and worrying away at it until he got what he wanted. When the softness of youth disappeared there was the makings of a very forceful, determined man. I'm glad I know him now, rather than later, Rowan thought, and then fleetingly, out of nowhere, she wondered what his father was like, and if Matthew took after him. She shook her head. She was getting too fanciful.

'OK, I give in.' It wasn't worth a fight. 'Since you'll be there you might as well come in and give a hand. But don't, whatever you do, say anything to the Press.'

'No, Doctor, ma'am,' Matthew grinned.

She grinned tiredly back. 'And watch the cheek!'

'Yes, ma'am.'

She sighed. He was incorrigible.

CHAPTER TWO

THE banging of a door brought Rowan's head up with a start, as footsteps could be heard pounding up the stairs near her room. It didn't sound like any of her colleagues, but who else. . .? The door to her room was flung open and for a second all she was aware of was a very tall, very dark, very angry man advancing on her waving a newspaper. Last night's meeting, she thought instantly. What can have gone wrong?

'What the hell's the meaning of this?' The paper was thrust under her nose. As she looked up into blazingly angry brown eyes, so dark they were almost black, she realised with a shock that her unexpected visitor was none other than Dr Nathan Pride himself. He dropped the paper on the desk before her and, his palms flat on the desk-top, leant forward, looming over her in a way Rowan could only describe as menacing. Tall herself, she wasn't used to feeling quite so intimidated as she pushed her chair back, rising quickly to her feet in an effort to get some control of the situation.

'Dr Pride, what's the matter?' She looked at him rather than the newspaper he was again pushing towards her. 'Please sit down, and maybe we can discuss whatever it is calmly.'

He was still furious, that much was clear, but she wondered whether it was a fleeting look of respect she saw briefly in his eyes. Whatever it was disappeared almost instantly as he spoke through gritted teeth.

'I want an explanation,' he ground out, one lean

forefinger stabbing at the newspaper, 'then we'll see about discussing things calmly.'

Since it was obvious he wasn't going to sit down Rowan picked up the newspaper, folded open somewhere in the middle, and reluctantly looked down at it. Her body froze as she took in the photo at the top of the page, her features taking on a mask-like rigidity as she sank back in her chair with a groan of disbelief.

'I take it you haven't seen the paper?' Nathan Pride was asking her, but she heard him as if from a distance and shook her head in an abstracted fashion, not taking in what he was saying.

Rowan's grey eyes widened and darkened as she focused on the photograph. A very clear, surprisingly flattering one of her, and an equally clear, equally flattering one of Matthew standing by her side, one arm apparently round her waist as he ushered her through an unseen doorway. She was turned to him, smiling at something he had just said, and they looked a very happy if slightly incongruous couple. The caption below the photo announced that it was of Dr Rowan Stewart and her new toy-boy secretary, Matthew Pride.

She registered the name and her eyes flew to the man before her. 'Pride,' she croaked through parched lips. 'Matthew Pride. . .'

'My son.' The uncompromising words were almost spat out, and Rowan could see that his anger, although under control, had not diminished.

'I don't understand. . .' She trailed off, then tried again. 'Your son?'

'Surely you realised when you *employed* him?' He gave the word an emphasis which suggested he would have preferred another word. 'After all, Pride isn't the most common of names.'

'He didn't use it.' Rowan was too dazed by the photograph and the brief, insinuating paragraph in the midst of the article about the research centre to do other than utter the bald truth, not even thinking of the possible implications.

Anger flared briefly in the man's dark eyes before dying to a blankness of defeat as he muttered, 'Didn't use my...his...name,' before rallying to demand, 'What name did he use?'

'Laurie,' Rowan answered, puzzled by the tightening of his lips as he heard the name.

'I see.'

Rowan was sure the name meant something to him, something unpleasant by the look of it, and wondered briefly what it could be.

'Then you didn't know he was my son when you...' He didn't complete the sentence, and Rowan was puzzled further.

'No, I didn't know whose son he was. Does it matter?' Having recovered from the shock of the photo, she was beginning to see the funny side of the situation and to enjoy it. Not so the angry man in front of her, who still wouldn't sit down.

'Of course it matters. He's done this deliberately to embarrass me.'

'Done what?' Rowan was growing more confused by the second.

'Taken this ridiculous job, and got his photo in the paper. With you.' His tone sounded very much as though he wanted to shout and was only restraining himself with difficulty.

Immediately Rowan bridled. 'It isn't a ridiculous job. It's a perfectly sensible, serious job, working for me as——'

'As a secretary. A woman's job!' The violence in

the words surprised her, but she began, at last, to understand what at least some of this was about.

'Don't you think that's a very sexist attitude?' As she spoke Rowan heard the echo of Matthew saying the same words to her, in that very room, and couldn't prevent a smile tugging at the corners of her mouth.

'And you needn't sit there smirking. I don't find the situation remotely funny, and neither will you.' The implied threat in his words was underlined by his tone and caused Rowan to throw her head back, a spark lighting her eyes. He wasn't going to get away with threatening her!

'And just what does that mean?' she asked in a deceptively gentle voice, the delicate planes of her face hiding her growing anger.

'I will not be made a figure of fun by my son being your secretary. Matthew isn't working for you any longer.'

'We'll see about that!'

The banging of the door in the next room silenced them both—a silence only broken when Matthew himself appeared at the connecting door enquiring in a cheerful voice, 'Coffee, Rowan?'

One look at him told her that he had seen the paper, and knew his father was there—and, what was more, was enjoying the whole situation. For a second she considered whether he had engineered the whole thing, but dismissed the thought as nonsense.

'You're not working here any longer.' Nathan Pride slammed the words at his son with all the subtlety of a charging rhino.

Matthew barely blinked, and Rowan wondered if he was used to his father shouting at him. The thought surprised her—she had Nathan Pride down as a cool, impassive man, sure of his own rightness, who wouldn't lower himself to lose his temper. He wouldn't think the other person worth it. Rowan drew up short at her thoughts — put like that she made Nathan Pride sound as though he was arrogant, conceited, with a selfish disregard for the feelings of others. Did she really mean that? Up until now she would have only agreed with the arrogant part, but now. . . Now she wasn't so sure. He seemed to be showing little regard for either her or Matthew's feelings.

'Is that what Rowan says?' Matthew looked at her, and for the first time Rowan really believed he was Nathan Pride's son. The colouring was lighter, less dramatic than his father's, but the steely determination sitting oddly in his puppy-soft eyes was the same. So was the stubborn thrust of his jaw. 'Are you sacking me?'

'No, of course not.'

The older man turned on Rowan. 'I told you I won't have him working as your secretary.'

'I can't, and I won't, sack him for that.' Rowan's voice was calm, although inside she was quaking. She didn't want to offend Nathan Pride — in fact, she couldn't afford to. He could make life very difficult for her, but it looked as though she had no option. 'It's something you'll have to work out between you.'

'And I'm staying.' Matthew leant against the doorjamb looking smug.

'Matthew!' His father looked ready to explode.

'You told me to get a job, and I got one.' Turning his limpid brown eyes from Rowan to his father, Matthew looked as though butter wouldn't melt in his mouth. Rowan almost expected to see a halo spring into shining existence above his curly head.

'Not this sort of job!' Nathan's temper seemed to be fading and now he sounded merely exasperated.

'What did you expect? I could always sweep the roads.'

'You could have found. . .' Nathan faltered.

'What?' Matthew was sounding belligerent.

'Something more appropriate.'

'How? You weren't going to help! Do it on your own, you said.'

Rowan was following the conversation with a growing sense of unease. There were things here that weren't being said, undercurrents that would make sense of the whole argument, if only she knew what they were. She latched on to Matthew's last comment. 'Is that why you didn't use your own name?'

'Yes.' Matthew looked sulky. 'The last part of my name. His name. Matthew Laurie *is* part of my name——'

'Matthew Laurie Pride,' his father interjected, 'and don't either of you forget it.' He turned on his heel and marched to the door, pausing to throw back at his son. 'We'll discuss this tonight.' Icy cold brown eyes, something Rowan hadn't believed possible, swept over her, bringing a dark red to her normally pale skin, but Dr Pride walked out without another word.

'You lied to me,' she accused, starting with the most obvious of all the things she wanted to say, to ask.

'No. I just didn't tell you the whole truth.' Matthew's grin was more a grimace. 'I used my mother's maiden name because I thought if you knew *he* was my father it would influence you in deciding whether to give me the job or not.'

'In which direction?' Rowan asked wryly.

'I wasn't sure.' Matthew had the grace to look slightly abashed. 'But I didn't want to get the job just because you felt you *had* to give it to me, or offend *him*. But neither did I see why I should lose it because of him either.'

'You thought I'd know he wouldn't want you to have it?'

'Not exactly. More I thought you might want to get back at him.'

'Good heavens, why?' Rowan was thoroughly taken aback.

Matthew shrugged. 'Don't know really. But I guess he offends a lot of people. He isn't very good at compromise.'

Rowan was dying to ask Matthew more, but suddenly realised that it probably wasn't very wise to pursue this conversation. She reverted to the main issue. 'Your father has made his feelings very plain. What do you intend to do?'

'Stay! If you'll let me.'

'I said a week's trail,' Rowan pointed out. 'Let's stick to that.'

'Great.' Matthew smiled happily, all trace of his sulky expression vanishing. 'Thanks. I won't let you down — honestly.'

'Hmm,' Rowan said non-committally. 'We'll see.'

As Matthew went belatedly to get them coffee Rowan watched his retreating back, wondering if she had done the right thing. She remembered their interview. Hadn't she guessed then that he wanted this job to get back at his father? And he hadn't denied that. But there must be more to it than resenting being told to get a job. Surely most students expected to do vacation work? And would it have mattered at all if he hadn't been Nathan Pride's son?

Why did she feel she was in the middle of a drama in which she'd missed the opening scene, and didn't have a cast list? And what was she supposed to have gathered from the scene just played? She picked up the paper that Nathan Pride had left and looked at the photo again. She didn't remember it being taken. Had Matthew known? And who had told the reporter he was her secretary? And Nathan Pride's son? *Had* Matthew set the whole thing up? And why? And clearly Nathan's relationship with his wife must have been acrimonious, if Matthew's use of her name could make him look so bleak when he heard it. Did he feel *Matthew* was rejecting him as well?

Making the coffee, Matthew smiled to himself. Step one of the great master plan had worked even better than he had hoped. And the Press meeting, complete with photographers, had been a heaven-sent opportunity he couldn't ignore.

'That's another fine mess you've gotten us into,' Anna said in a poor imitation of Oliver Hardy.

'What's with the "us"?' Rowan asked despondently, running slender fingers through her thick, wavy blonde hair. She had confessed all to her friend in the hope of some support and sensible advice. Some hope from a consultant psychiatrist, she thought cynically.

'If Nathan's angry with you, he's not going to be very happy with me either, is he? You know how we get paired together in people's minds because we do so much research together.'

'I suppose so. Sorry.' Rowan hardly sounded sorry, but that didn't bother Anna.

'Doesn't make a lot of difference. I was hardly flavour of the month with our Nathan as it was.'

'Why don't you like him?' asked Rowan. It suddenly struck her that her friend really *didn't* like Nathan Pride, but was covering it by pretend dislike. She was using jokes to cover her real feelings.

'You'll blow a fuse if I tell you,' said Anna.

'So?'

'And I shouldn't really.'

'When has that ever stopped you before?' said Rowan drily.

'Swear you won't repeat it?'

'Do I ever?'

'When we were interviewing for the new consultant's post he made a comment about not wanting another woman. Said something about having our token woman consultant and not needing any more!'

Rowan was as outraged as Anna had know she would be. She was also speechless. So much for Dr Nathan Pride. He was even more chauvinistic than she had expected. But why that should depress her so she couldn't understand.

'I didn't know you saw patients here.' Nathan's voice might be frosty, but at least he had spoken. It wouldn't have surprised Rowan if he had walked past her without speaking, without acknowledging her existence in any way. The end of the trial week had come and gone, and neither she nor Matthew had raised the subject of his leaving. But both were under no illusions about how angry Nathan would be.

'I have a meeting with the nurses who are running the patient groups,' she replied, relieved that he appeared to want to be civil, if not friendly. Bad feeling between them could cause problems. That she had more personal reasons for not wanting to have a bad relationship with Nathan Pride she didn't dwell on. Her thoughts were preoccupied with him all too often these days. It was something she would have to squash. There was no reason, no reason at all why Nathan Pride should mean anything to her. Until the last couple of weeks she had hardly been aware of his existence. Matthew's entrance into her life might have led to some increased contact with Nathan, if his storming into her office could be called that, but there was no reason why their paths should cross again.

Whether he would have said any more Rowan wasn't to know, as a clatter of heavy boots sounded along the corridor and two young men swung into sight. Both had dark, curly hair and such a striking resemblance to each other that they could only be brothers. Both were dressed in jeans and leather jackets, but whereas one was clean, tidy and presentable, the other was scruffy and looked as though he had been sleeping in his clothes.

'How ya doin', Doc?' The younger, more dishevelled of the two lurched towards Rowan, his movements jerky and uncoordinated. She stood her ground, a smile crossing her face, as at the same time she realised Nathan had tensed beside her. She wondered briefly if he thought there might be trouble. She knew she was in no danger from Danny MacNamara, but that Nathan might be concerned on her behalf was a pleasingly comforting thought.

'I'm fine, Danny, how are you?' Her smile encompassed both youths and she added, 'Hello, Iain.'

'Morning, Doctor.' The lines of strain in the young man's face smoothed slightly as he returned the smile with genuine warmth. They both turned to look at his younger brother, who was shadow-boxing—at least, that was what it looked like. Both knew that Danny was convinced he was in constant battle with Janna, Lord of the Outworlds. Sometimes Danny was really fighting his delusional adversary, other times his shadow-boxing was no more than that—practice. This looked like one of those times.

'Things are a bit heavy at the moment,' Iain told her, 'but he's up to get his jag this morning. Maybe that'll calm him down a bit.'

'Tell him I don't need no jag,' Danny instructed Rowan, while he continued to aim jabs into the air with both fists. 'There's nothing wrong with me.' He pivoted with balletic grace to aim a punch into the air behind him. Rowan didn't bother to reply, knowing that he wasn't really listening and that anyway she wouldn't be able to convince him of his illness.

'You a doctor?' Danny's punching abruptly ceasing, he turned his attention to Nathan.

'Yes.' Sliding his hands into his trouser pockets, Nathan met the youngster's gaze unblinkingly.

'A psychiatrist?'

'Yes.'

'I haven't seen you before.'

'No.'

'Psychiatrists — you're all the same.' Danny launched into an impassioned tirade against all doctors, his language becoming fouler by the second. It was nothing new to either Rowan or Iain, who had heard all this from Danny before. Nathan Pride's impassivity indicated that he had been on the receiving end of such outbursts before as well. None of them interrupted or tried to disagree.

'Sorry about that.' Iain gave them both an embarrassed grin as Danny lurched off down the corridor towards the depot clinic. 'I'd better get after him.'

'See you, Iain,' Rowan called after him, as Nathan silently watched the two men's progress down the corridor.

'You seem to know them well,' he remarked.

Rowan shrugged. 'Iain's one of the best. The rest of the family have pretty well given up on Danny, but

Iain keeps on going. He even takes time off work to make sure that Danny comes for his injections.'

They both knew that many patients with schizophrenia didn't like getting the depot injections that would help control their symptoms. They also knew how necessary they were.

'It can't be easy,' said Nathan. 'He's not much more than a lad himself.'

'Twenty-three,' Rowan confirmed, 'and Danny's twenty-one. Iain drives a mini-cab, which gives him a bit of freedom with his hours to deal with Danny. I think he resorts to strong-arm tactics to get him here sometimes, but it's probably worth it. Danny's symptoms are at least liveable with now.'

'Hmm.' Nathan's non-committal grunt echoed Rowan's own feelings. Things might be better than they were, but they still weren't easy in the MacNamara household. Life with a person acutely ill with schizophrenia could be disruptive to say the least.

'It puts one's own problems into perspective, doesn't it?' Rowan uttered the words without thinking their impact through and realised, as she watched Nathan's face harden into grim lines of controlled anger, that he thought she was making a not-so-subtle reference to his head-on collision with his own son. That had not been in her mind when she had spoken so unthinkingly, but to say so would only make matters worse, she reflected. It didn't surprise her when, with a stiff nod of his head, Nathan walked away without saying another word.

Damn! Why did she always put her foot in it? And just when she thought they might be able to put the issue of Matthew working for her behind them.

* * *

'You seem remarkably jaunty today.' Matthew, normally bright and cheerful, today was acting like a puppy who had found a particularly juicy bone. His good humour seemed almost tangible.

'Dad's away for a week!' He couldn't keep the excitement out of his voice. 'So I've got the house to myself.' His grin threatened to split his face.

'I hope you'll be sensible,' Rowan cautioned, as she had visions of a gang of eighteen-year-olds running riot through Nathan's home. She knew from the address Matthew had given her that they lived on the outskirts of the city, and the houses there were big, old and elegant. She shuddered to think what might happen if Nathan came home to find Matthew had been having wild parties.

'Don't you start. I've had enough lectures on responsibility from Dad.' Matthew pulled a grimace of distaste, but then immediately grinned again. 'I don't need to do anything wild to enjoy myself. Just not having him breathing down my neck all the time is enough. Living with him's like a gaol sentence.'

The underlying bitterness in his young voice couldn't be completely disguised, and left Rowan with a sense of unease. From a few comments Matthew had let slip she had gathered that he had only recently come to live with his father, having been with his mother since the separation. Piecing the bits together, she had deduced he would continue to live with his father while he was at university. She had also gathered he wasn't at all pleased by that prospect. At first she had supposed he missed his mother, but somewhere along the line Rowan realised that as much as Matthew might say he disliked his father his feelings for his mother were even more negative. What Nathan felt about it all she couldn't begin to guess—only that the adjustments both were having to make were no easier for the older man than the younger.

By Friday Rowan thought Matthew's good humour was slightly forced. It was only when she asked him if he was looking forward to the weekend and caught a glimpse of strong emotion before he could hide it that she realised that something was wrong.

'Got something exciting planned?' Rowan persisted, and as she spoke she had a sudden insight. Why had it never occurred to her before? Matthew was lonely. If he had only recently come to live here he couldn't have many friends.

Matthew shrugged. 'Not really.' He sounded so bleak that for a moment Rowan had an overwhelming surge of anger towards Nathan and a strong need to tell him exactly what she thought of him going off on holiday and leaving his son at home alone.

'Didn't you want to go on holiday with your father?' she asked, wondering if she was pushing her luck and Matthew would any minute tell her it was none of her business.

'Dad's not on holiday,' Matthew informed her with a hint of surprise. 'He's gone to a conference in London and is then going on to see some colleagues of his about the genetics stuff. Oxford, I think. Or maybe Cambridge.'

'Don't you know where he is?' Rowan was appalled. 'What happens if you need to get hold of him urgently?'

Matthew looked slightly shamefaced. 'I've got a list of phone numbers. I just didn't pay any attention to what he was saying.'

Rowan let out a long breath. Nathan wasn't quite as uncaring as she had supposed.

It wasn't what she had intended to do with her evening, but her kind heart got the better of her. 'Well, if you're not doing anything tonight, would you do me a favour?' she asked.

'You want me to work late?' The lightening of Matthew's expression was enough to convince her she was doing the right thing. If he could look that pleased at the prospect of overtime then things must be bad. Her heart went out to him.

'Not exactly, no.' She took a deep breath and hoped this was the right thing to do. 'I really want to see the new Harrison Ford film and I don't have anyone to go with. Would you like to come with me? We could grab something to eat first and . .' She didn't finish as the look of relief on Matthew's young face told her how much the suggestion meant to him.

'Great idea,' he told her, as he rushed to hold the door open for her. 'I'm yours to command.' He grinned again. 'Do you think people will think you're out with your toy boy?'

Rowan wordlessly shook her head. She wasn't at all sure that Nathan would approve of her going to the cinema with his son, but she wasn't prepared to leave Matthew on his own.

Matthew breathed a sigh of relief. Step two was well under way.

'Are you doing anything tomorrow night?' Matthew asked as they left the cinema. 'Would you like to come to dinner?' The words came out in a rush and Rowan realised that Matthew had had to nerve himself to ask. 'I've been learning to cook since I've been living with Dad, and I need someone to practise on.' He sounded so forlorn that Rowan didn't have the heart to refuse him.

'Are you sure you can put up with me again?' she teased, and was worried by his immediate reply. He was a nice lad, fun to be with, but she didn't want him getting any ideas. I must be mad, she told herself; I'm twelve years older than him—he couldn't possibly think anything of it. He was just bored and lonely. And she felt sorry for him.

'Oh, yes! I really like spending time with you, Rowan.'

She didn't see how she could refuse now without appearing rude or that she was rejecting him. And there was another consideration. She'd get to see his house—Nathan's house. She had always been of the firm belief that you could learn a lot about a person from seeing where they lived, what they chose to surround themselves with. And for some reason she refused to analyse she wanted to know as much as she could about Nathan Pride. The chance to see Nathan's home, while he was away, was too much to resist.

CHAPTER THREE

'COME and join us, Rowan.'

Rowan turned to see who was speaking to her, recognising the voice but being unable to place it immediately. It was with something like surprise that she saw Professor Robbie Scott waving her to his table. Even more surprising was the man with him—Nathan. She hadn't realised that the two men were in the habit of lunching together. It would have been odd if they didn't know each other professionally, but the comfortable body posture of each hinted at a more personal relationship. The thought made her uneasy.

As she moved to join them Rowan wondered whether fate had been kind to her when some unknown force had prompted her to go into the university staff club for lunch. Normally she rarely ate there, leaving the dark wood and slightly stuffy atmosphere to the older members of staff. And the department being based in the nearby hospital rather than on campus would make going there a special trip. But for some reason today had found her feet leading her in that direction almost of their own accord as she walked back from a trip to the library. There was no way she could turn down an invitation from her head of department, supposing she wanted to. Even so, this lunch could be difficult in more ways than one. She looked at the packet of cheese sandwiches and the apple on her tray. How was she going to crunch her way through an apple with any semblance of dignity—or, more important, retain any degree of attractiveness? As she put her tray on the table in the space the two men made for her she noted, with relief, that both men had apples. At least they were all in this together.

'You know Nathan, of course.' Robbie Scott beamed beatifically at Rowan, his head bobbing between them like a small, cheeky bird.

'We've met,' Nathan acknowledged non-committally, but Professor Scott either did not notice or ignored the neutral tone, and the merest hint of a warning.

'Of course, of course.' His smile grew, if anything, broader. 'With Matthew working for Rowan you're bound to.'

Rowan ground her teeth silently together as she mentally took Matthew to task. So much for his blithe comment about introducing himself to Professor Scott, who had seemed 'surprised' to see him. I'll bet he was surprised, Rowan thought darkly; her boss obviously knew Matthew well.

'Matthew's my godson,' Robbie told her confidingly, causing Rowan's heart to drop even further.

'Really?' was all she could manage to utter, totally dumbfounded by the revelation. Matthew, she silently berated him, wait till I get my hands on you. Hot on the heels of this came the even more disturbing thought — And what else haven't you told me?

'He's grown into a fine lad,' Robbie told Nathan, as though his father didn't know. 'You must be proud of him.'

'Yes.' The single word was uttered more tersely than was strictly polite, and Rowan took pity on Nathan. He obviously didn't want to talk about his son with her, and Robbie Scott looked set to launch into a series of family anecdotes. The least she could do was head her boss off.

'I didn't realise you knew each other so well,' she threw in, hoping it would get Robbie away from the topic of Matthew, but prove sufficiently interesting for him to pick up. Robbie wasn't usually one to give up a good topic for stories without a fight. A quiet little voice whispered to her that by picking that subject she might also learn something about Nathan. There was even an outside chance that Matthew's mother might be mentioned.

'Why should you?' Nathan said quietly, almost under his breath, but not so quietly that she didn't know she was supposed to hear, and that Robbie wasn't. Immediately she regretted having wasted any time and effort on trying to spare his feelings.

'I suppose not,' Robbie was saying, 'but I remember Nathan as a medical student when I was a very new registrar — although it wasn't medicine that first brought us together——'

Nathan was looking even more cold and distant, if that was possible, and once again Rowan felt a twinge of sympathy for him. It looked as though Robbie was about to be indiscreet.

'Maybe you shouldn't tell me,' she interrupted laughingly. 'I'm sure anything you got up to then is going to be embarrassing for someone.'

Nathan looked sharply at her, and she wondered if he was surprised to hear her talk like that to her boss. But Robbie was used to it. He favoured informality all round and not infrequently counted on his staff to get him out of situations into which he had so blithely and unconcernedly walked.

'You're right,' he laughed delightedly, 'so I'll spare both our blushes.' He leant conspiratorially towards Rowan. 'But get Nathan to tell you some time. He comes out of it much better than I do.'

And that was what was so nice about Robbie Scott and saved him in most circumstances, Rowan reflected. He was a fun-loving man who was quite happy to tell stories against himself, and if he embarrassed others sometimes more often than not it was because he showed them in a kinder and more generous light than they were used to.

Glancing again at the two men, obviously firm friends, she was struck by the disparities between them—Nathan so tall, dark and, it had to be said, handsome, and Robbie none of those things, but nevertheless an attractive man. At five feet nine Rowan topped her boss by several inches. His chubby form was topped by a mass of tight sandy blond curls and the pale blue of his eyes was usually matched, as it was today, by the pale blue of the bow-tie he habitually sported. He looked nothing like anyone's idea of a successful professor of psychiatry, but exactly like everyone's idea of a teddy bear brought to life. Next to his good-humoured exuberance Nathan seemed colder, more aloof and more arrogant than ever. But that Robbie was clearly prepared to count him a good friend of many years' standing was a very definite plus point in Nathan's favour, Rowan conceded reluctantly.

As she watched Nathan covertly out of the corner of her eye she was pleased to see that he appeared to be relaxing. Maybe he realised that she was not going to probe Robbie for any details of his private life, his hidden secrets. Briefly the thought surfaced that she could pump Robbie, at a later date, for information about Nathan's wife, but rejected it. She could no more ask Robbie than she could Matthew. If she was going to learn anything about Nathan it would have to come from him.

As though realising that he was losing out to Robbie in the charm stakes Nathan turned to Rowan, his practised smile slightly less forced than it had been as he focused the full impact of his high-voltage eyes on her.

'How are the patient groups going? I trust you've managed to smooth out last-minute problems?'

So it was going to be like that, was it? Rowan thought. Polite talk about work, civil discussion and nothing remotely personal. Fair enough. She even liked the idea of describing Henry Munro as in need of smoothing, but wisely stuck to more practical, administrative details.

If she was going to be fair to him, and she was doing her best to overcome her prejudice, it had to be said that he showed an apparently genuine interest in her work, and Rowan felt herself relax the tension that had been a tight band between her shoulders, keeping her perched uncomfortably on the edge of her chair. Nathan also relaxed, his face losing some of the harsh lines from nose to mouth as animation smoothed them out, replacing them with lightly etched laughter-lines fanning out from the corners of his eyes.

It was as they laughed ruefully together at the vagaries of the hospital's records department that Rowan realised Robbie was being uncharacteristically quiet. A quick glance showed an unusually grave expression at war with his habitually naturally cheerful features. When he noticed Rowan's questioning gaze he relaxed his expression, but although he joined in the general amusement Rowan noticed that he still looked very thoughtful.

Rowan had just bitten into the despised apple when Robbie leapt to his feet with a muttered exclamation and a garbled explanation about being late for a meeting. With no more apology he hurried away, cramming his own apple into the pocket of his baggy jacket. Rowan glanced at Nathan's apple. The last thing she could imagine him doing was spoiling the elegant lines of his immaculate tailoring by stuffing an apple in his pocket.

'Don't let me keep you,' she suggested, 'if you have to go,' hoping he would take the hint.

'Not at all,' he responded blandly, 'I'm in no hurry.' And suiting action to words he too picked up his apple and, elbow resting on the table, bit into it with perfectly even white teeth.

As the two of them chewed thoughtfully Rowan cast about for a suitable topic of conversation, but none were forthcoming as her mind stayed worryingly blank. She took another bite of apple, the crisp, crunching sound echoing noisily to her ears, despite the hubbub of conversation around them. They couldn't just sit there and eat their apples without saying a word. It was just too silly. She had to find something to say. As she searched a still vacant mind it was Nathan who broke the conversational void.

'How's Matthew getting on?' he asked.

It was the last topic she had expected from him; indeed it was the very one she had been so assiduously avoiding.

'Very well,' she mumbled through the mouthful of apple, struggling to appear unconcerned by either the question or the steady gaze now directed at her, and knowing she wasn't succeeding.

'Are you sure?' Nathan persisted, leaving Rowan to wonder what this inquisition was about. She had thought that an uneasy truce existed between them over Matthew's job. What existed between Nathan and his son she didn't begin to know.

'You're not just being polite? Or humouring me?' The lightness had faded from Nathan's face, but he looked concerned rather than aloof, serious rather than arrogant. Like any father with a genuine concern for his son's welfare, she recognised. It was a thought which caused her some concern. She was developing a growing fascination with Nathan Pride and it was disconcerting to remember that he was Matthew's father, especially when Matthew's mother was such a total unknown.

Her thoughts drifted back to Saturday night and her visit to his house—a visit she was convinced he knew nothing about, and, as a consequence, a visit she felt increasingly guilty about. The old house was beautifully, and impersonally, maintained by a housekeeper, but for all the splendour of the antique furniture it looked more like a grand country-house hotel than a home. The dark colours and lack of flowers or any other feminine touches proclaimed it as a masculine household. There had been no photographs anywhere, Rowan had discovered, her avid eyes searching for some insights into Nathan's personal life. Glad to see that Nathan didn't keep a picture of Matthew's mother on display, she was still disappointed not to know any more of the woman. Nathan's wife—ex-wife, she had discovered that much—was an enigma, and Rowan recognised that she was becoming preoccupied with finding out more about the woman—starting with what she looked like. Of course, she had only seen the hall, kitchen, dining- and living-rooms. Finding herself suddenly wondering what Nathan's bedroom was like, she found herself blushing hotly as she met his quizzical gaze.

'*Is* everything all right with Matthew?' he asked

again, something in his voice telling her he was steeling himself to receive an unfavourable reply.

'Yes, really,' she insisted. 'He's an absolute godsend. I know the job's pretty much a game to him, but he's still doing very well and being a tremendous help. If I'm honest, it's working out very much better than I could have hoped.'

There was an almost imperceptible sigh from Nathan as he released a pent-up breath, and Rowan realised just how important her testimony had been to him. She wondered if she dared risk a question.

'Does he seem to be enjoying it to you?' For a second she thought she had gone too far and Nathan wasn't going to answer. Then he laid his apple on the plate and, resting one arm on the table, leaned forward.

'Very much,' he astonished her by saying quite calmly. 'I'm surprised by how hard he seems to be working and, quite frankly, I didn't expect him to last more than a week. After he got the predicted response from me I thought he'd tire of the job and give it up.'

'Is that why you responded as you did, hoping he'd leave?' Rowan hadn't thought him quite that Machiavellian but was, by now, prepared to believe practically anything of him.

His grin was rueful, and very, very slightly sheepish. 'I'm neither that devious nor that clever! It was only *after* I'd blow up that I wondered if that was what he'd been hoping for.' He shrugged. 'I'm still not sure that I approve of him working as a secretary, but I have to hand it to you—you've certainly got him involved. He's always been a bit flighty in the past—doesn't stick with anything very long. He certainly doesn't stay with anything that needs effort.'

Thinking back to the boy's very impressive record

of academic achievement at school, Rowan thought that wasn't quite how she would have described Matthew, but it didn't seem politic to contradict his father.

She did, however, say, 'I think the credit goes to Matthew. He's working very conscientiously.'

'Good.' Nathan smiled at her, the warm, totally sincere, gratified smile of a parent whose offspring had, for once, done something of which to be proud. As she returned it, happy to have been able to bring him that pleasure, their eyes met and held. Rowan became aware of her smile fading in tune with Nathan's as tension built between them, the air burning with a sudden electric charge. Her mouth suddenly dry, she found herself once again speechless, only this time it looked as though Nathan was also struggling to find something to say.

'Maybe I owe you an apology.' The tone of the hesitant, softly spoken words was enough to tell Rowan that Nathan was as caught up in the spell of the moment as she was.

'Nathan, I. . .' She faltered to a halt, not knowing what she wanted to say. Or maybe realising that what she *did* want to say couldn't be said. Not now. Not yet. Her eyes dropped from his mesmerising gaze to focus on his large, well-shaped hands, the pristine whiteness of his shirt cuff, the black leather of his watch strap, the clear white of the watch face, the time.

'The time!' Galvanised into movement, she looked up and caught a flash of unguarded and unrecognisable emotion in Nathan's eyes, quickly disguised as their eyes met again. 'I'm sorry, I have to go — Outpatients.'

With that she almost ran from the dining-room, not daring to look round, not wanting to know if Nathan had already forgotten her and gone back to his apple, and yet unwilling to face him if he was watching her hasty departure.

'Do you think it would help?' Although she had very strong feelings about what would and would not help the patient in front of her Rowan was trying to get the young woman to make some decisions for herself.

'Aye, I suppose so.' Mary McFadden sounded less than optimistic, but it was a start. There was a long silence as the woman struggled with herself and eventually reached some sort of decision. 'Aye, I'll give it a go. What have I got to lose?'

What indeed? wondered Rowan, looking at the slightly overweight woman before her — a woman who was exactly ten days younger than Rowan herself and who looked at least ten years older.

'I'm worried about making things worse again,' Mary added. 'I don't want them voices back.'

'I don't think that will happen,' Rowan told her, 'but we'll all be keeping a careful look-out for signs of relapse. You as well,' she pointed out. She had been explaining the patient education groups to Mary and was getting a grudging agreement from her to attend.

'Aye.' Another silence stretched. 'What I *really* want——' Mary broke off, as though surprised to find herself stating any wants.

'What do you want?' Rowan hid her delight. Mary was usually so passive that she never made any demands. But to show too much excitement might be enough to put more pressure on her than she could comfortably deal with. Rowan sent up a quick, silent prayer that Mary's 'want' was within the bounds of possibility and something she could do something about.

'I want to lose this weight I've put on!' The words came out in a defiant rush, and Rowan muttered a quick thank you under her breath. It wasn't an easy request, but neither was it totally impossible. 'It's them drugs—I know that's what's made me blow up. Everyone else at home is thin. . .they go on about it . . .all the time.'

That was the heart of the problem. Rowan wondered anew at the insensitivity of some families. Here was Mary, recovering from a second schizophrenic episode, and all the family could do was to go on about her weight.

'They don't help, I grant you that,' she agreed. 'Have you talked to Dr MacDonald about them?' She knew Anna was planning to take Mary off drugs altogether soon, so there was no harm in raising the issue now.

'Aye. We thought we'd give them a break and see what happens.' Mary didn't look convinced. 'But if it means having the voices back I'd rather stay on the drugs and stay fat.'

'Given your history, Mary, there's a very good chance you can come off the phenothiazines and still stay well,' Rowan explained, 'although we'll keep an eye on you, of course. This last episode was fairly short-lived, and you've recovered remarkably quickly.'

'Aye.' Mary was still less than convinced. 'Will I lose weight as soon as I stop the drugs?'

'Probably not. I think you'll have to make a bit of an effort to lose the weight.' Rowan saw no point at the moment in pointing out to Mary that, as well as weight gain being a side-effect of the drugs controlling her schizophrenia, she had seen the other woman eating a constant stream of chocolate bars, biscuits and cakes which were also contributing to the problem.

Carbohydrate craving as a side-effect was one thing, what Mary was eating was something else again. And her passivity meant that she moved as little as possible and certainly didn't take anything resembling exercise. It was hardly surprising she had put on weight.

'There's a new weight group starting at the day hospital in a couple of weeks. Do you want to go to that?'

Mary nodded vigorously. 'Aye, that'd be grand.'

'I'll put your name down and send you the details.' Rowan was pleased. Mary sounded more enthusiastic about that than anything she could remember.

Mary took her leave, and as Rowan wrote up the notes she found herself dwelling on the differences between them. I have so much to be thankful for, she told herself firmly. So why do I feel so. . .empty?

Just recently she had been forced to admit to herself that her work, exciting and fulfilling as it was, wasn't enough any more. She had friends, a close, loving family, but for no apparent reason, and quite out of the blue, she had begun to wonder if she was lonely. The more the thoughts persisted, the more she found herself wondering about Matthew's role in this.

The more she saw of Matthew, the more she was aware of a restlessness, a part of her that had been ignored for too long. In vain she tried to remember whether the feelings had existed before his eruption into her life, whether he had only highlighted something that was there already, or whether she had only become conscious of the lack after his advent. And why should it be Matthew stirring these feelings into life? she questioned.

She was very fond of him. He was a nice, bright, attractive boy, she admitted that freely, but the emphasis was on boy. She couldn't seriously be attracted to him, could she? Unlikely as it seemed, she knew that for some reason she was drawn to him. It's nonsense, she insisted. He's little more than a child. A bit lost, a bit lonely. . . Her thoughts trailed to a stop. Maybe that's the answer, she thought; you've picked up Matthew's feelings and they've struck a chord in you — so much so that you've started to identify with him. It's nothing more than a reaching out to someone with whom you have compatible feelings.

Relief washed through her like a cleansing tide. If that *was* the answer it was something she could handle, could deal with. She wondered if Matthew sensed the same feelings in her, and that was why he said he felt so comfortable with her. Whatever the explanation, she knew she had to be careful of their growing friendship. She could just imagine Nathan's reaction to Matthew developing a crush on her, or the hint of any relationship between them.

Nathan! Where did he fit into all this? *Did* he fit into this? He was a very attractive man, but Rowan couldn't envisage ever feeling at ease with him. There was an indefinable something that kept her on edge whenever he was about. Was it only her relationship with Matthew that caused the tension between them, or were there other contributors? Despite his comments at lunchtime Rowan knew he was still unhappy about Matthew working for her. Why should that matter?

The knock on the door saved her from further speculation as the next patient arrived.

By the end of the afternoon she had found two patients who she thought might be of interest to Nathan for his genetics study. Dougal MacLaren came originally from the Western Isles, but had been living for a number of years in Glasgow with his aunt. From a large family he had several relatives he described as 'odd' still living in the Islands, two of whom had been diagnosed schizophrenic.

Then there was Jamie Cameron. Not only was he diagnosed schizophrenic but he had an older brother at home also diagnosed schizophrenic. His father's oldest sister had been in a psychiatric hospital for many years and his grandfather was an acknowledged eccentric. Jamie thought he had been in hospital at one time, but since the death of his wife ten years before he had cut himself off from everybody and lived pretty much as a recluse. The family visited now and again, keeping the house clean and making sure there was a supply of tinned food in, but he took almost no notice of them.

'He has the voices for company,' Jamie explained, as though there was nothing unusual in this. Reflecting on the family history, Rowan had to agree that for him there probably *wasn't* anything odd in his grandfather hearing voices.

Having obtained both patients' permission to pass their names on to Dr Pride, Rowan was eager to let Nathan know of the families. That her enthusiasm was less motivated by academic or clinical interest, and more by a desire to talk to Nathan, she chose to overlook. Now that she had a cast-iron excuse to phone him she wasn't going to let that go to waste.

It was late afternoon when she got back to her office, and Matthew had already left. Collapsing into her chair, Rowan eased her feet out of her shoes, swinging her chair round to catch the early evening sun still streaming through the windows. The bright green of the trees across the road dappled the sunlight as it fell across her face, a rippling pattern of light and shade soothing her tired mind.

The pile of messages Matthew had left for her beckoned and she picked them up, only to let them drop in her lap as she leant back and shut her eyes. It would be so easy to sit there and fall asleep. With a monumental effort she forced her eyelids open and swung the chair back to her desk, compelling herself to look at the messages. Unless anything really urgent presented itself they could all wait until tomorrow.

It was the third piece of paper which really caught her eye and arrested her attention.

'Dr Pride called. He'll phone again tomorrow.'

The message was unexceptional—then why her unease? Matthew could hardly have written 'Dad phoned', could he? Then why did the message look so accusatory?

There was nothing for it but to ring Nathan and find out what he wanted. Part of her believed, indeed hoped, that Nathan would have already left and wouldn't be available. Her accelerated heart-rate and rapid breathing told a different story. She wanted every opportunity she could get to talk to Nathan, get to know him. The memory of his dark, compelling eyes formed in her mind as she dialled his number with slightly shaky fingers. The hospital switchboard answered with unaccustomed swiftness, and before she knew it she was connected with his extension, the hammering of her heart almost drowning out the ringing of the phone.

'Pride.' The rich bass voice broke into her chaotic thoughts with a suddenness which left her momentarily speechless. His, 'Hello?' was rapped out with an abruptness hinting at a busy man annoyed with both the interruption and then being kept waiting by someone who didn't know what he or she wanted to say.

'Er—hello. It's Rowan Stewart. You left——' She

stumbled over the introduction, but was cut short by Nathan, his tone becoming warmer, more friendly.

'Rowan. Thank you for ringing back. I thought I'd missed you for the day.' He sounded so pleased to hear from her that Rowan's heart thumped even more rapidly. Don't build your hopes up, she insisted to herself. It doesn't mean anything. He probably wants information, or to tell you something about one of the patients. It's nothing personal, nothing to get excited about.

'It occurred to me,' Nathan was continuing, obviously oblivious to the pounding of Rowan's heart which was deafening her, and which she was convinced must be travelling down the phone lines to similarly deafen him, 'that it might be useful for you to know more about the genetics work if you're going to describe it to patients.'

'Yes, of course.' She had to say something, although so far there was little need, if only to prove to herself that she could still speak.

'I'm going out to do a family interview this evening, and to take blood. I thought you might like to come along.' It was a perfectly ordinary, perfectly reasonable suggestion, so why did Rowan think there was more to it than that? Surely it was her imagination that there was something in his voice, a warmth, an uncertainty, that had nothing to do with an ordinary, reasonable suggestion about work.

Dampening down her immediate response of 'I'd love to,' Rowan sought for something more prosaic and businesslike.

'That's a good idea. It would be helpful. What time are you going?' The last was added in an effort to sound busy and professional. She had nothing organised for the evening, and even if she had she would have changed any plans to go with Nathan—even if it was only to visit patients.

'I'm leaving in about half an hour. Shall I come and pick you up?'

'Yes. Thanks.' Her mind was whirling. If he took her home it would mean leaving her car in the car park overnight. That wouldn't matter... Having hung up, she worried for a few minutes that she should have told him she would meet him there, that she had her own car. But she hadn't, and it was too late now to be concerned over his interpretation of what she had done. He needn't have offered her a lift at all.

Nathan held the car door open for her in an old-fashioned gesture of courtesy which made Rowan go weak at the knees and, admitting it ruefully to herself, undermined her more feminist tendencies. It was one of the reasons she had always steered clear of any involvement with anyone she worked with. Maintaining a coolly competent professional image and not getting a reputation for using feminine wiles was important. A man like Nathan made that very difficult. His masculinity was a forceful, all-pervasive aura, so powerful that it was almost impossible not to respond to him as a man rather than a colleague who just happened to be male. To her utter disgust Rowan was even aware of a desire to flutter her eyelashes at him— a desire which was squashed firmly as she forced herself to ask questions about the interviews and the family they were going to see.

By the time they pulled up in front of a neat semi in the suburbs of Glasgow Rowan had a potted history of the Murray family, a fairly clear understanding of the interview schedule Nathan was using and an outline of the format of the session.

'It would be helpful if you chat to whoever else is there while I ask each of them some questions in private', he told her. 'Most of the interview can be conducted as a group effort—it helps to get things clarified if they go over the family history and connections together. There are always debates about who's who and how they're related.' He smiled across at Rowan, fine lines fanning out round his eyes. 'We all assume we're absolutely clear about our families, but when we come to describe it to a stranger it's funny how many discrepancies creep in.'

Mrs Murray, a small, plump woman with a beaming smile, had the door open for them as they walked up the path to the house between immaculately manicured flower-beds, and started talking even before they reached her. Barely giving Nathan time to introduce Rowan, she led them into the sitting-room, which was filled almost to bursting-point with people.

Rowan recognised Simon Murray as the patient, having seen him around the hospital a few times, and then Mrs Murray was introducing her clan. As well as her husband and two other children, one with his wife, there was her sister with her husband and two teenage children, a brother who 'lived down the road' and another brother, his wife and daughter.

'They live in England now,' Mrs Murray explained, 'but when I told them about this research of yours they decided to come up and see you for themselves.'

Rowan darted a quick glance at Nathan to see how he took to being described as one might a new, exotic pet, but realised that his slightly stunned expression had more to do with the number of people than Mrs Murray's garrulousness. Presumably he was used to that.

Tucked away in the corner of the room were Mrs

Murray's parents, Robert and Hester Buchan, looking slightly dazed themselves by their loudly vocal family.

Recovering quickly from his surprise, Nathan rapidly launched into a short speech of thanks, cutting off Mrs Murray's ramblings in a manner that, by her lack of offended response, that lady was well used to. Taking charge, he set Rowan to drawing up a preliminary family tree while he took blood samples from all the descendants of the Buchans.

The interviewing bordered on the farcical at times, but Rowan knew they were getting useful information. For all her talkativeness Mrs Murray was well organised and the matriarchal figure which kept the family together. She had contacted various aunts, uncles and cousins, getting permission from them for Nathan to contact them and persuading them that they should go to their GPs to give a blood sample 'for this important research'.

As Rowan and Nathan emerged from the Murrays' nearly two hours later, somewhat shell-shocked and full of tea and scones, they exchanged conspiratorial smiles but, by tacit agreement, said nothing until they were in the car.

'Is it always like that?' Rowan shook her head, trying to clear it, her ears still ringing from the babble of sound. Nathan grinned at her—not a smile but a real grin, making him look years younger and much, much more approachable.

'Hardly,' he laughed, 'but I shouldn't complain. Someone like Mrs Murray is an absolute godsend in this research. She's the keeper of the family history and does so much of the work for me. I can arrange with the GPs to take the bloods, but it's Mrs Murray who'll get the family there.'

'Her organisation is certainly impressive,' Rowan

acknowledged, looking at the detailed list of names, addresses, phone numbers and relationship to one another that Mrs Murray had given her.

'What I really find impressive about these families,' Nathan mused, 'is that there's nothing in it for them, yet they go to so much trouble. They know it's "research", that it might help pin-point genetic linkage in schizophrenia, but that's it. They know it will do nothing for them, and their current predicament, but still they go to all this effort.'

They drove in silence for a couple of miles, then Nathan said, almost too casually, Rowan thought, 'It was very useful having you there tonight. If you have time maybe you could come with me on further interviews.'

'I'd love to.' The words rushed out, not quite in the way Rowan had intended to express herself, but Nathan didn't appear to notice anything untoward.

'Good,' he said.

'It must be difficult doing them on your own,' she remarked.

Nathan shifted in his seat at that and Rowan thought he looked slightly uncomfortable.

'Er — my registrar usually comes, but it's not always convenient.'

Rowan's heart sank. He only wanted her to fill in when someone else wasn't available. Anyone would do. This idea was scotched by Nathan himself adding, 'And I think it's time we got to know one another better, don't you?'

'Yes.' The word was so softly spoken that Rowan wasn't sure if she had said it aloud, but her spirits were soaring again. Not wanting to read too much into it, she concentrated on work and remembered she hadn't told him of the two possible candidates for the project she had discovered that afternoon.

'Unfortunately, I have another engagement now,' Nathan told her, 'but phone me tomorrow with the details and we'll meet to discuss it.'

CHAPTER FOUR

THERE was no reply from Nathan's extension the next morning, and all his secretary would say was that he couldn't be disturbed. When this happened for the third time Rowan took the hint. Tempted as she was to not give him the details he would need to track down Dougal and his family, she rose above such petty childishness, telling herself that just because Nathan was in a huff about something or other it didn't mean she had to respond in like manner. Thus it was with a self-satisfied feeling of virtue that she replaced the receiver and turned her attention to Matthew.

In the past three weeks she had come to believe she knew him fairly well, and his manner this morning suggested that something was preying heavily on his mind. She had hoped he would tell her of his own accord, but it was beginning to look as though she would have to prise it out of him. Leaning back in her chair, she stretched, pushing her heavy blonde hair away from her face, running long, slim fingers through to lift it away from her neck before letting it fall free. There were times when she wished she had never met either of the Pride men, and today was fast turning into one of those times.

'You're not going to like it,' Matthew warned her, when she had finally got him to admit that there *was* something troubling him.

Rowan's already despondent spirits drooped further. Maybe she should forget all about it, ignore it.

'Does it concern me, and am I going to find out

anyway?' she asked. There was the faintest flicker of hope at the back of her mind that the whole thing might just disappear.

'Yes, and yes,' Matthew responded gloomily. The day, Rowan decided, was getting worse and worse by the minute. Better to get it over with now; the day was already spoiled. Leaving it might only ruin another day.

'You'd better tell me, whatever it is.' Her voice matched her expression, and neither gave Matthew any sense that she was going to easily forgive him his part in the mess.

'I don't know why I told him.' Matthew collapsed into the chair on the other side of Rowan's desk, looking totally defeated. Against her will Rowan felt a stirring of pity for him. It was easy to forget just how young he was. Whatever mistake he had made, he was certainly sorry about it. She primed herself to be bracing and deal with the matter quickly. The last thing she needed was Matthew moping around looking tragic, like a bit player in *Hamlet*.

'Told who what?' she demanded, the unexpected authority in her voice causing Matthew to sit up straighter and look more alert.

'Dad——' he started, stopping at Rowan's gasp and sudden loss of colour, leaving her naturally pale skin ashen. Somehow she had avoided contemplating that the source of Matthew's problem was his father. It had been so much more comfortable to focus on work-related issues.

'Rowan? Are you all right?' Matthew looked even more worried, the frown creasing his normally smooth brow emphasising his resemblance to his father.

'As right as I'll ever be with you working here,' she informed him with undue bitterness, and was immediately sorry at the hurt which flooded his eyes. How come such a normally strong, cheerful young man could, so suddenly, look like a kicked puppy? she wondered. It simply wasn't fair.

'I'm sorry, I didn't mean it. It's been a bad day so far,' she apologised, not needing to add, And it's getting worse by the minute. The unspoken words hung between them. 'Tell me *exactly* what this is about.'

'I told Dad that we'd been to the cinema together last week, and that you'd come out to the house for dinner,' said Matthew.

'You did *what*?' Galvanised into action, Rowan jumped to her feet before realising that there was nothing she could do, and sank back down into her seat. 'From your expression I gather he wasn't pleased.' She looked at Matthew, knowing he would confirm her statement, but hoping against hope that he wouldn't.

'You could say that.' From Matthew's tone and deadpan expression her description of Nathan's reaction was quite obviously an understatement of the first order. 'He said——'

'I don't think I want to know,' Rowan cut him off, understanding now why Nathan hadn't returned her calls, wouldn't speak to her on the phone. But she didn't think she could bear to hear from Matthew what he really thought of her.

'He'll tell you himself, anyway,' Matthew reported miserably, then went bright red as he remembered just how forcefully his father had expressed himself. Surely he wouldn't say *all* that to Rowan?

'What?'

'He said something about seeing you,' Matthew mumbled, looking, if it were possible, even more despondent. To see him look so defeated touched Rowan's kind heart, and she decided he. . .they. . . were making too much of it.

'OK, I can appreciate the fact that your father might not be very happy that I visited his home without his knowledge or invitation——' As she said the words aloud Rowan acknowledged that maybe she had been very silly to give in to the impulse to see Nathan's home, and maybe he did have some right to be annoyed, '—But I'll apologise, and that will be that. He can't actually *do* anything, can he?' She hoped the latter comment sounded more like a statement than a question. What Nathan might do if he took it into his head to get even wasn't something she dared contemplate.

'I suppose not.' Matthew's face clearly indicated that the words were said more because he knew she expected them than from any sense of conviction.

'Right. Let's forget about it, then, and get down to some work.'

It was easier said than done, but Rowan felt she owed it to Matthew to set a good example. Despite her best efforts as the day progressed her mind kept worrying away at the question of what kind of father Nathan was. Matthew seemed unduly worried by the storm he had whipped up with his unwise revelations. What on earth was he expecting Nathan to do?

Ward 6A housed a group of female patients who had been in hospital for at least five years, most of whom had been diagnosed schizophrenic, and who were now being prepared for resettlement in the community. The ward was officially designated a 'rehabilitation ward', but not everyone wanted to leave. It was

Rowan's turn, with Jenny, the occupational therapist, to field questions in the weekly discussion group.

'The housing department hope to release two flats soon,' Jenny reported. 'They'll need to be redecorated and furniture sorted out before anyone can move in.'

'I want a pink bedroom.' Maggie had been reiterating her desire for a pink bedroom from the moment it had been suggested she leave hospital. Everyone was getting a bit fed up with her constant talking about it. 'Pink walls, pink ceiling, pink carpet, pink bedspread, pink——'

'Everyone will get to choose colours for their own room when we decide who's going where——' Rowan cut across Maggie's list of coveted pink objects, knowing full well that she was capable of going down to the smallest detail of comb and tissues for at least half an hour, given the opportunity.

'Sounds awful,' Pat, the youngest of the group, broke in, voicing her opinion loudly. Although privately she had to agree, Rowan stepped in to keep the peace.

'Everyone has their own ideas and taste,' she pointed out tactfully.

'It'll be like living in a bowl full of blancmange,' Pat persisted, and Rowan noticed that Jenny was also struggling to keep a straight face. But when she looked around at the drab green of the hospital walls, which had been Maggie's only home for the last ten years, it was easier to understand the other woman's desire for colour and a pretty, feminine bedroom. It represented the freedom of choice to do exactly what she wanted, no matter how over the top — a freedom from all decisions being made for her, as happened in institutional living.

'Not all the same pink,' Maggie informed them

loftily, 'different shades. Light and dark. See?' With a flourish worthy of any magician she produced a large piece of card from her even larger handbag. It was covered with little squares of pink paper stuck neatly in rows — and, indeed, the pinks varied.

'What's that, then?' Pat went to snatch the card away, but Maggie held it out of her reach, giving it to Rowan to examine.

'I was telling Dr Pride about the pink bedroom I'm going to have,' she informed them haughtily, 'and he said maybe I could collect sa...samples...yes, samples of the sort of different pinks I'd like. So I did.'

'What a lovely idea.' Rowan was delighted with Nathan's suggestion, and not just because of what it had done for Maggie. That such an intensely masculine man should find such a solution for his patient showed Rowan just how deeply committed he was, how much he really cared for the person behind the patient, no matter how aloof he might be with the rest of them. Nothing was going to stop Maggie daydreaming about her bedroom, nor talking about it, but this was a way of channelling that preoccupation into something they could all deal with. She forced her misty eyes to focus on Maggie's colour chart.

'Maggie, this is absolutely wonderful!' Rowan was delighted and amazed at the care the woman had put into the work, and wondered if Nathan had known that Maggie could produce something like this, or whether it had simply been chance, an off-the-cuff remark to stop her diatribe about pink.

'This is really clever,' Jenny offered, looking at the card over Rowan's shoulder. It was considerably more sophisticated than either woman would have expected, the squares of coloured paper cut from magazines and neatly set on the page, each labelled 'Walls', 'Carpet',

'Sheets' and so on as appropriate. The shades complemented each other, and Rowan began to believe that a wholly pink bedroom might not be the total disaster she had envisaged. Feeling guilty at how easy it was to fall into the trap of underestimating the long-stay psychiatric patients, Rowan passed Maggie's card round to be duly admired and exclaimed over before going back to the more pressing business of setting up visits for the women to go and inspect the flats which would become their new homes.

As she pulled the fuchsia pink baggy cotton T-shirt over her head Rowan's thoughts drifted back to Maggie's pink bedroom. Far from being shocking pink, or even the sickly chewing-gum pink that Rowan had assumed she meant, Maggie's chart of intended colours ranged from palest pearly pink to a deep, rich coral. Looking around her cool blue and grey bedroom, Rowan discovered that maybe her choice of décor was just a bit arctic.

The doorbell sounded loud in the silent flat as she adjusted the T-shirt and she looked down at the long length of her bare legs. Having no idea who could be calling on her in the early evening, she hurriedly thrust her legs into immaculate white jeans as the doorbell sounded again. She was still fastening them as she crossed the hall in her bare feet to answer the door. Whoever was on the other side was displaying a marked lack of patience and was, to all intents and purposes, leaning on the bell as it continued to peal through the otherwise silent flat.

Whether it was Matthew's warning or the persistence with the bell, Rowan was not altogether surprised to find Nathan Pride on the other side of the door. She was, however, surprised to see him looking quite so angry. From what Matthew had said she had supposed that with a quick apology to Nathan she would be able to charm him out of his annoyance. She hadn't counted on this, however. Nathan was far from being just annoyed. He was furious! There was nothing of the charm he had shown last night, nor the controlled arrogance with which he dealt with professional matters. Now he was nothing more and nothing less than a raging male animal.

Without greeting her, or waiting for any greeting from her, he pushed past her into the flat. Automatically Rowan closed the door behind him, only afterwards realising that it might have been more sensible to leave it open. With the mood Nathan was in she wanted to speed him on his way as quickly as possible. Leaving the door open would have, at the very least, been a strong hint that she didn't want him to stay.

She never even got the chance to ask him what he wanted, for, without giving her any opportunity to speak, Nathan launched into a venom-laden speech.

'I have only one thing to say to you, Dr Stewart, and that is *leave my son alone*!'

'What?' the comment as well as the tenor of his words threw Rowan into confusion. She had thought that he accepted Matthew working for her, even if he wasn't exactly happy about it.

'You heard me. I want you to leave Matthew alone.'

'I told you that if he wanted to work as my temporary secretary that was up to him. You'll have to sort this out between you. It's none of my——'

'I'm not talking about his job, unsuitable as it is,' Nathan snapped, 'and well you know it. Don't try any red herrings——'

'Wait a minute.' It was Rowan's turn to interrupt him. 'If it's not the job, then what on earth are you talking about?' Her genuine bewilderment stopped Nathan in his tracks for a second, a guarded look crossing his dark face as though he was assessing her for some suspected, devious behaviour.

'I am talking,' he told her deliberately, articulating each word with slow care, 'about the dates you've had with my son. About the fact that he's totally besotted with you, and that you seem to be encouraging him.'

Rowan's lovely mouth fell open with shock. Surely he couldn't be serious? He couldn't mean. . . Could he? She went cold at the thought, and gave an involuntary shiver despite the warmth of the evening.

'I see you have nothing to say in your defence.' The satisfaction she might have expected to hear in his voice was strangely absent, and for a moment Rowan received the distinct impression that Nathan had expected her to strenuously deny everything. It was only then she realised she hadn't said a word.

'I'm not sure that I understand what you're suggesting,' she informed him coolly, holding on to her rapidly escalating temper and hoping he would take the opportunity she was giving him to withdraw his snide insinuations. 'But I'm sure you're wrong about Matthew's feelings about me. And I'm damn sure you're wrong about my encouraging him.' Her anger, slow to kindle, had been building up while he had been speaking and erupted with the last sentence.

They faced each other in the spacious hall with enough distance between them to make them look like boxers waiting in their respective corners for the bell to sound. That a fight of some sort was starting Rowan had no doubt. Her major concern was that there was no referee to hand.

'You're not going to deny that you went out with

Matthew last week, are you?' Nathan slammed the question at her, sure of the response.

'No, but——'

'Or that you told him you had no one else to go with?'

'No, but——' Rowan wondered what else Matthew had told his father. She hadn't realised he had included so much detail. It seemed such an odd thing to do. What had he been thinking of? If he wanted to stir up trouble it was the best way to go about it.

'You're years older than him. What the hell do you think you're playing at? He's only a boy, and——'

'Stop right there, Dr Pride, before you say something we'll both regret.' Rowan was struggling to gain mastery over her temper, and the authority in her voice and the quiet dignity in her bearing as she held down her wrath were enough to silence Nathan in midsentence.

'Let's get several things straight. Matthew is not a *boy*, he's a young man, and it's time you treated him as such. Secondly, I'm very fond of him, and I believe he's fond of me. But that's between us and nothing to do with you. Thirdly, yes, I invited him to go to a film with me. I see nothing wrong in that. In fact——'

'I hadn't realised you were so hard up for escorts.' Nathan had also regained some control while Rowan had been speaking and, apart from a slash of dull red across his high cheekbones and a barely perceptible shortness of breath, he was once more in total control. 'I'm surprised.'

'I don't know——' His words caused Rowan to lose track of her arguments, and she floundered to an embarrassed halt under the very close scrutiny of Nathan's suddenly blazing eyes.

He took a step nearer her. 'You're a very lovely

woman, Rowan,' he told her almost impersonally. 'I'm surprised that there aren't, if not hordes, at least a couple of more suitable. . .men who'd be happy to take you out. I would have thought you were rather wasted on a lad like Matthew.'

The supercilious tone, coupled with the way he was looking down his well shaped if fractionally too large nose was enough to make Rowan see red. For all that her ash-blonde hair, pale complexion and grey eyes gave the outward appearance of cool competence and icy control, she had an impetuous streak and quick temper which matched the copper colouring of her father.

'How dare you? If I really thought you could believe one preposterous word you've said I'd. . .I'd. . .'

'You'd what, Dr Stewart?' Nathan relaxed as Rowan's show of temper gave him the upper hand. 'If you're intending to slap me, and I do think that would be a bit melodramatic, you'll need to stop flapping your hands about like that first. You need more control to —'

'Oh, you —' Slapping him hadn't crossed Rowan's mind, but now he had put the idea there it seemed a very good one. Drawing her hand back in readiness, she found her wrist grasped in Nathan's strong grip as he forced her hand down to her side. The movement brought their bodies close together, and as she bent her neck back to look up at him she fully comprehended, for the first time, not just how tall he was, but how much strength was packed into his muscular frame.

'Now, let's talk about this calmly, shall we?' His warm breath fanned her cheek, causing it to flood with colour at the same time as her heart speeded up. He's doing this deliberately, she thought, knowing that his fingers on her wrist would be aware of her rapid pulse. She tried to pull away, but he held her fast. Short of an undignified struggle which she was certain she would lose, it seemed that she had to submit. There was, however, still the refuge of anger.

'What is there to talk about?' She forced the words out from behind clenched teeth, all the time wanting to scream, Let go of me. But she wasn't going to give him the satisfaction of asking for that only to have him deny her, demonstrating his control over her.

'Why are you so interested in my son?'

'I'm not. At least, I'm very——'

'—fond of him. So you said. I still want to know why you need to set your sights on a boy. If you're that hard up for an escort I'd be only too happy to take his place.'

'Why don't you, then?' Rowan didn't know who was the more shocked by her words, Nathan or herself. Nathan immediately dropped his vicelike grip on her wrist, but in the stunned silence that followed neither moved. Rowan couldn't take her eyes off the smooth white cotton of his shirt front and the sombre subtlety of his dark silk tie as she kept her gaze firmly cast down, unable to look up and meet his eyes. She was sure she would read amused triumph mingling with contempt there. As her fixed gaze never wavered she also noticed the motion of Nathan's chest, indicating rapid breathing, and became aware of the shallow speed of her own.

'Rowan——' Her name shattered the silence as his husky voice cracked on the single word, but it was enough to break the unconscious hold he had on her, and she stepped away, turning her back on him as she raised both hands to burning cheeks.

'I don't know why I said that. It must have been the anger of the moment. Please forget it.'

'And if I don't want to?' There was something oddly taut about his voice and his face, she saw, as he gently turned her to face him.

'It would be best if you did.'

'Let me be the judge of that.'

Why was he pursuing it? Surely it was as embarrassing for him as it was for her? What sort of game was he playing with her? She still couldn't believe that he really thought she was interested in Matthew.

'Nathan, please leave.' Her use of his Christian name was unconscious. She couldn't think of anything else to say and didn't know how defeated she sounded — nor how that touched Nathan in a way her anger could never have done.

'I'll go now,' he agreed, 'but I'll be back in an hour to take you to dinner.'

Blinking rapidly, Rowan held on to her composure for all she was worth as the hall swam dizzily around her. Shock was piling on shock, and it was more than she could stand. Taking a deep breath, she forced her voice to sound natural.

'What sort of joke is this, Nathan?'

'No joke. You're the one who threw out the challenge, Rowan. I'm merely picking up the gauntlet.' He walked to the front door, intent on letting himself out. As he opened the door he turned back to her. 'Judging by your current state, you're going to need more than an hour to get yourself together.' He glanced at his watch. 'Shall we say half-past eight?' He didn't wait for any reply but shut the door quietly behind him.

Matthew watched his father leave for his date with Rowan barely concealing his glee. For all the difficulties of their relationship he loved his father and wanted to see him happily settled with a new wife, even a new family. And he knew there was no way his father would marry one of the glamorous, empty-headed clothes-horses he normally dated. Not understanding what had set his father so totally against remarriage, Matthew had decided to do something about it. He had noticed Nathan make several comments about a certain Dr Rowan Stewart, seemingly in passing, and always connected with work, but something in his tone of voice alerted his son. Nathan might not be aware of any interest in her yet, but Matthew was sure it was there. She was so unlike his father's usual girlfriends that Matthew was convinced it would never occur to his father to date her. Trying to find out about the woman, he had questioned his godfather, Robbie Scott, and it had been Robbie who had mentioned the job with Rowan. It was then that Matthew had hatched his plan for the summer, naming it, with more than a little dig at his father, 'Pride's Fall'. Now it looked as though his machinations were going to pay off.

The west-end restaurant was comfortably full, the hum of conversation rising and falling as a background music that only served to make Rowan uncomfortably aware of how stilted the conversation was between her and Nathan. To ease the tension which was holding her body rigidly on the edge of her seat she reached for her glass of wine, but as she raised it to her lips she knew she wouldn't be able to swallow, and put it down again. Her anxiety caused her hand to tremble so that the rich red liquid swirled around the glass. Alternately she cursed Nathan for being difficult enough to suggest this dinner and herself for being weak enough to accept. Nervous fingers stroked the stem of the glass, twisting round and round, until the wine threatened to spill over the top. Realising what she was doing, and how much she was betraying her feelings, she let go of the glass with such suddenness that it would have toppled over but for Nathan's quick action which had it safely restored to the upright before she fully realised how close an accident had been.

'Sorry.' The word slipped out, acknowledging not just her clumsiness but her tension, her unease with the situation.

'I'm sorry too.' Nathan's quietly spoken words confused her. What had he to be apologising for? Her perplexity broke the barrier of anxiety and, without thinking, she raised her eyes to meet his, and was further mystified by the warm amusement glowing in their dark brown depths, like the bright embers of a burning peat fire. Before she could ask her question he answered it, causing her to wonder if he could read her mind.

'I'm sorry you're so on edge, that you feel so uncomfortable here with me, but I'd be lying if I said I was sorry I forced you into having this dinner with me. That's one thing I'm *not* sorry about — not if you can learn to unwind and feel more comfortable with me.'

'Why——?' Her voice cracked, high-pitched, on the word, and she took a steadying breath and tried again. 'Why did you invite me to dinner?' She hoped the question sounded more casual than it felt, but her hands betrayed her nervousness as her fingers once again crept towards her glass, intent on nothing more than fiddling with it. In this they were deflected as Nathan's strong, tanned hand covered hers, enfolding her fingers in his, stilling their agitation.

'There are a dozen reasons,' he told her, running his thumb caressingly over her wrist.

'Name one.' Breath catching in her throat made her voice husky and her pulse was on the increase again in response to Nathan's tantalising touch.

A wry smile twisted his lips, almost as though he felt she was calling his bluff, which, to some extent, Rowan thought she was. She was sure he had flung out the invitation—order, more like—in an unguarded moment of anger. She was equally sure that he wouldn't be honest enough to admit to that. But she would know, and he would know she would know. And somehow, she thought to herself, that should give her an edge over him.

A slight weariness touched the corners of his smile, dulled the bright fire in his eyes to a steady glow, but he didn't let go of her hand. Instead he turned it over and gazed down at it, almost, Rowan thought bemusedly, as though he was going to start reading her palm. That fanciful notion was instantly dismissed as he threaded his fingers through hers and looked up again to meet her wide, surprised eyes.

'Because I like having dinner with a beautiful woman,' he informed her, his voice matter-of-fact but his eyes saying so much more.

'Oh.' Rowan felt cheated. The fact that he had described her as a beautiful woman was almost lost on her in the well-nigh impersonal tone he used. Some of her disappointment showed in the clouding of her grey eyes and the very slight downward curve of her lips.

'I could give you more reasons,' he confided softly, 'but you only asked for one.'

'Yes.' Her whole arm seemed to be tingling from his touch. His fingers were still entwined with hers, his thumb running lightly backwards and forwards over the inside of her wrist, shooting a sharp awareness of him through her body.

'Do you want to hear the others?' he asked, his deep velvet voice dropping even lower.

'Yes,' said Rowan, who had meant to say no, who knew she should pull her hand away from his and restore some order to her pulse, her breathing and her thinking.

Nathan's half-smile seemed to her fertile imagination, to reach out to enfold her, and she felt warmth spread through her, and her fingers exerted a pressure on Nathan's almost of their own accord. It was as though her fingers did not belong to her. But the answering pressure from him coursed through her, drawing a response from every part of her body.

'I said I like having dinner with a beautiful woman, and you, Rowan Stewart, are very beautiful. You grow more beautiful every time I see you. I find myself thinking of you at the oddest times, and I don't like having my concentration interrupted in that way. I know so little about you, and I want to know more. I want to know everything, and then maybe you won't intrude into my thoughts.'

Rowan winced inwardly. He sounded almost distanced from what he was saying. She didn't doubt the truth of anything he said—either that he did find himself thinking of her, or that it was against his will and he wanted to be rid of such annoying thoughts. But she had to pay attention to what else he was saying.

'Matthew talks about you—all the time, it seems. I was so angry with you that you could disregard my wishes and allow him to continue working for you. But then I discovered I was pleased that you'd stood up to me. I was annoyed and—yes, and upset that you acted as though you wanted to keep me at a distance, that you were uneasy in my presence, and I wanted to change that. I want to change that very much.'

He raised his hand, still holding hers, so that both their elbows were resting on the table and she was inevitably drawn forward, to lean towards him. He dipped his head slightly to brush warm, dry lips across her knuckles.

'But most of all I was angry at your preferring Matthew to me.'

'But I. . .I. . .' Rowan was bereft of all speech. The situation had escalated out of any control she might have been able to exercise, and she wondered if any sense of control she had experienced had been mere delusion fostered by Nathan.

'It seemed to me you did,' Nathan explained, taking her stuttered interruption for denial. 'You took his side against me over the job, you're at ease in his company, you appear to enjoy spending time with him, so much so that you even went out with him. I was angry, but I was also hurt. And jealous. And I didn't like feeling jealous of my own son, a mere boy. I want to get to know you better. I want you to enjoy spending time with me. I want you to feel at ease with me. That's why I invited you out to dinner.'

'Oh!' If there was anything more sensible to say it escaped Rowan at that precise instant. Nathan's glowing eyes held hers, his lips were curved in a soft, seductive smile, his rich voice flowed round her like smoothest silk and the touch of his fingers sent shivers running through her. Sincerity oozed from him, and his words confirmed her earlier thoughts. He was jealous of Matthew. Why, then, much as she wanted to believe him, did she still feel uneasy? Why did she feel he was telling the truth, or some of it, but using it, bending it to suit some purpose of his own? A nameless purpose that made her feel very, very apprehensive — like an insignificant fly being drawn into the carefully constructed web of a very skilful, very crafty spider.

Without warning Rowan remembered Anna's throw-away remark about Nathan's string of glamorous girlfriends. How many others had sat opposite him, probably in this same restaurant, and been seduced by his honeyed words and apparent sincerity? Disappointment threatened to overwhelm her, and she blinked rapidly to dispel the awkward onrush of tears.

'Nothing to say, Rowan?' Nathan asked, still softly, his eyes never leaving her flushed face.

'You have no reason to be jealous of Matthew,' she said, realising the truth of that statement. 'The idea's preposterous.'

'And you'll try to feel more at ease with me?' he persisted.

'I don't not——' She began to deny his observations, and then realised she couldn't get away with the denial as his eyebrows arched upwards in amused disbelief. 'Yes, I'll try.'

'Good.' There was satisfaction in his voice, but something more. Something that made Rowan believe she might have misjudged him, that he didn't have an ulterior motive for his confession. Something that made her want to get to know Nathan very much better indeed.

CHAPTER FIVE

'YOU went out to dinner with my father.' Matthew confronted her with his knowledge, sounding strangely accusatory.

'Yes.' Striving to stay cool, Rowan almost groaned aloud. Another jealous male was almost more than she could bear. Matthew's frown deepened at her simple affirmative and he nodded to himself, as though confirming dark, hidden thoughts.

'Rowan, it's none of my business, but——'

'No, it's not.' It was the first time she had been so abrupt with him, telling him in no uncertain terms that there were boundaries to their relationship and he was about to cross one of them. She didn't want to hurt Matthew, but the memory of Nathan's slow, lingering kiss as he said goodnight was enough to push all other considerations aside. Nathan was a fascinating, exciting man, and against that her desire to spare Matthew's feelings stood very little chance.

'—but I care about you,' Matthew persisted, determinedly ignoring Rowan's remark, 'and I don't want to see you hurt by my father.'

'Matthew, I——'

He cut her off, clearly determined to say what he thought he must. At some point in the night Matthew had got cold feet about his plan. His father's self-satisfied smile when he returned home reminded Matthew of his ever-changing string of girlfriends—and his mother's constantly reiterated denunciation of Nathan and his abominable behaviour. Not that

Matthew had really believed this, but a startlingly new protectiveness towards Rowan had him wondering whether he had done the right thing in trying to bring her and his father together. He had finally confessed his plan to his godfather, who told him he was playing with fire. 'Dad—well, Dad isn't. . .I mean. . .I don't think he means to do it intentionally, but. . .well, I don't know how to put this, but. . .'

'Then maybe you shouldn't.' Rowan tried to stop Matthew's urgent if disjointed torrent of words.

'I have to. Dad's girlfriends never last long. He seems to get fed up with them quite quickly and then just dumps them. I don't want him to do that to you.'

Rowan was touched by the concern Matthew was showing and, if not alarmed, unhappy at his confirmation of what she had already deduced.

'First of all, Matthew, I'm *not* your father's girlfriend. And, secondly, I don't think we should discuss him,' she said firmly.

'But——'

'I appreciate your concern, but there's really no need.'

'But you need to understand why——'

'No, Matthew.'

'But——'

'Drop the subject, Matthew.'

There was no denying her tone of voice. Matthew, having no option, let the matter go, but Rowan, knowing his tenacity, wondered unhappily when, and how, he would raise it again. If Matthew had something he wanted her to hear she had no doubt but that she would end up listening.

Rowan walked along the pale green institutional corridors without seeing them. She was still puzzling over

Matthew's reaction to her dinner date with his father. His attitude was a strange, ambivalent mixture. Part of him seemed to be genuinely pleased that she had met with his father. Presumably he saw a more affable relationship between his father and his boss as a way for his life to become more pleasant. It couldn't be easy for him, Rowan thought, knowing how plainly Nathan had made his feelings known about his son working for a woman in what he still persisted in calling 'a woman's job'. On the other hand, Matthew was clearly troubled by the idea of an impending relationship between Rowan and his father. Rowan wondered just how much his warnings were real and how much were nothing more than sour grapes.

Matthew couldn't be jealous, surely? Her mind twisted away from the idea, unwilling to face the possibility that Matthew could have read anything in their relationship other than friendship. The idea that Matthew might have misinterpreted her overtures was unsettling, but even so it was less worrying — or maybe that should be more comfortable to worry about — than the thought which was valiantly straining to push its way to the surface of her mind. And that was, when was she going to see Nathan again? Or even, *was* she going to see Nathan again? Despite his tender leave-taking he had made no mention of repeating the experience. Had she been *so* boring over dinner? Or maybe it was that she had goaded him too far and he had simply picked up the challenge she had so rashly issued, and then lived to regret it.

Whatever had happened she had no business thinking about it now, she told herself sternly. She was here to work, and her time and energy would be better spent on that than worrying about the two Pride men, who were both more than capable of taking care of themselves.

The rehab group was ready and waiting to start when Rowan arrived, and a quick glance at the wall clock informed her she was several minutes late. She must have been dawdling in the corridor unforgivably for her to have lost so much time. Another black mark went against Nathan as Rowan blamed him for the persistence of her thoughts.

With the unpredictability of large bureaucratic organisations the two flats had suddenly been made available for the women, after everybody had been led to believe there would be a delay of months. Both flats needed work doing to them, so it would still be some time before the women could move in, but the knowledge that the flats were waiting was all the impetus they needed to really get down to work.

'Pink,' Maggie was chanting under her breath, 'pink, pink, pretty pink, pink.'

'Thank God I won't have to put up with her rambling much longer,' Pat remarked, glowering at Maggie from under lowered brows.

Rowan glanced at Jenny, the OT, and neither said anything. Both could sympathise with Pat's sentiments.

Pat didn't fit the pattern of the other women in the group, being, at twenty-three, much younger, and with a less chronic problem. For all that, she had had a severe psychotic episode, although she was functioning well now. She had been living rough when she had been brought into hospital, having been thrown out of her bed-sit a couple of weeks earlier for rowdy behaviour. With hindsight it was obvious that that had been the beginnings of her schizophrenic episode, but there had been no one to notice, or to care, at the time. She had left home when she was seventeen, not long after her mother had remarried, claiming she didn't get on with her stepfather. Although her mother kept in touch she refused to have her daughter back to live with them, and Pat, just as adamantly, refused to go. Between them, Rowan and Jenny had persuaded her to go into one of the group flats rather than live on her own. To their surprise that had been easier than they had expected, and Rowan felt sure that Pat missed being part of a family and was secretly looking forward to creating a cosy domestic camaraderie with the other women.

Not all group flats were single-sex, but for one reason or another these women had reason to distrust men, and Pat had seemed to fit in well with them and the slight anti-male stance of the group. It made Rowan wonder even more about Pat's stepfather and her real reason for leaving home.

They were midway through a rather heated debate about how much they should tell the neighbours about themselves when one of the few popular members of the unpopular sex walked in, taking them all, not least Rowan, by surprise.

'Dr Pride. Is anything wrong?' Jenny was immediately on her feet, flustered and obviously wondering what on earth could bring a consultant to their group meeting.

'I've just been told about your flats and came to offer my congratulations and good wishes to you.' His smile encompassed the entire group.

His effect on the women was electric. Each of them sat up that bit straighter, patting her hair or smoothing her dress or otherwise making the normal, small feminine gestures that such a very male man produced on any group of women. Rowan noticed that even Pat flicked a finger at her spiky hair standing up straight away from her head, and hid a secret smile to herself. It was all so *normal*, so reassuring. They were behaving like women, and not like patients.

Her mouth twisted in a wry grin which she could not conceal as she acknowledged that she was behaving like a psychologist and not a woman, noticing the effect Nathan had on the others so that she herself did not have to react.

Catching Nathan's eyes on her, she saw an eyebrow raise questioningly as he noted the rueful curve of her lips. What he made of it obviously left him less than pleased as his brows creased together under Rowan's wondering gaze.

His features smoothed again to bland politeness as he turned back to the group and asked formally if he might join them, if no one minded. Since he was already pulling a chair forward Rowan had a sudden urge to say yes, she objected, just to see what he would do. Realising that she would be shouted down if she tried, she wisely kept silent.

The women were vying with one another to tell him of their plans, and Rowan felt a growing sense of concern. Despite squabbles and irritation among them from time to time they co-operated well together and generally presented a pretty united front to anyone from outside the group. All it took was one good-looking man to have them competing with one another for his attention.

It was Maggie who dropped the bombshell.

'Pink,' she interjected loudly into the general babble of conversation, and then, when she had got Nathan's attention, 'You can take me to get the paint now. Pink paint.' She produced her card with its colour swatches and held it to her like a talisman.

Nathan looked as though he wasn't sure he had

heard Maggie correctly. Or wasn't sure the remark had been addressed to him.

'Maggie, I don't think Dr Pride can——'

'Said he would,' Maggie interrupted Jenny, 'when he told me to do this.' She waved her card aloft.

Nathan looked stunned, as well he might, as he fully took in what Maggie was saying, and Rowan thought she could almost hear the wheels of his mind whirring away as he tried to remember *exactly* what he had said to Maggie.

'Who's going to take us?' Dora, one of the other women, wanted to know.

'Dr Pride could take us all,' another joined in.

Rowan wasn't altogether surprised to hear Pat mutter under her breath, 'Dr Pride can take me any time he likes.'

Let's see him worm his way out of this, she said to herself, delighting in what she was sure was his discomfiture. As she met his eyes across the group she couldn't prevent the tiniest hint of a triumphant smile curving her lips upwards.

Jenny was already trying to quieten the group and explain that Dr Pride couldn't possibly take any, let alone all of them, when he cut across her somewhat disjointed utterances.

'I think it's a splendid idea,' he said, taking the wind out of Rowan's sails completely. 'But we'll need more than one car, and I know nothing about paint and things.' He looked directly at Rowan. 'Dr Stewart will have to come as well.'

'What are you playing at?' They had left the group at the same time, and now, quite forgetting herself, Rowan caught at Nathan's sleeve, holding him back when he would have walked away from her.

His dark, well-shaped brows shot up as his eyes dropped to focus on her hands, clutching the fine wool of his immaculate and expensive suit. Despite herself Rowan felt the hot colour flood her cheeks as she hastily let go of his arm, but she wasn't going to let him get away without an answer.

'Do you know what you've just done?' she demanded. She wouldn't have believed his eyebrows could ascend any further, but they did, giving his surprise at being taken to task an almost comical element.

'I appear to have annoyed you,' he returned imperturbably, the eyebrows descending slightly as he almost shook his head with bemusement at the woman standing before him. 'But I'm not sure why. Surely you don't begrudge the time to take these women to the shop for paint?'

A dark cloud passing over his face told Rowan how little he would think of her if she admitted to this. But the time involved was not among her problems.

'Of course not.' She dismissed the notion instantly, and was rewarded by the slight clearing of Nathan's shadowed brow, although he was still regarding her with a hint of cynicism. 'But what you're suggesting just isn't on!'

'And why not?' The cold, haughty tone was every inch a consultant who didn't expect to be taken to task by junior staff and told his ill-thought-out plans were unworkable.

'Things don't work like that—you must know that. Where's all the money going to come from, for a start?'

Nathan's head gave an abrupt jerk while his eyes narrowed to regard the woman challenging him more closely, and his was enough reaction to have Rowan triumphantly gloating to herself, for a second at least. She *knew* he hadn't thought any of it through and had rushed into speech to get at her in some mysterious way.

'I understood there was money set aside for the redecoration of the flats.' Nathan spoke slowly, covering up the hesitancy Rowan was sure he was feeling as it became clear that he really didn't understand how these things worked. Her sensation of triumph was short-lived, however, when she remembered the women patients. She and Nathan had to get themselves out of this mess with least upset to the patients.

Instantly she abandoned her plans of dragging out Nathan's unwilling display of ignorance of the system, adding fairly to herself that he had no real need to know all the ins and outs. And just as quickly she launched into her explanation.

'The new tenants get some say in colours and so on, but the work's done under contract. I assume paint's bought in bulk as there are only a few standard colours available. Everything has to be done as cheaply——' she grimaced '—or should I say as cost-effectively as possible. We've never been able to take patients out to choose things or to. . .well to just be able to spend real money.'

Rowan was disconcerted to see the frown back between Nathan's brows fiercer than ever. 'But the money is there, isn't it?'

'Yes, I suppose so. At least, on paper,' she added.

'Well, then?'

'I've no idea how to get at it. Nor, I suspect, has Jenny. Things have always been done like this, and the accountants——'

'Then things can change!' Nathan exclaimed.

'But——'

'No buts. Leave it with me.'

He walked a few paces along the corridor, leaving Rowan staring after him in confusion, before turning round and saying softly, 'Trust me, Rowan,' which had the effect of leaving her even more confused than before.

Trust me, he had said, but in what? To sort out the problem he had inadvertantly created over the women's shopping trip, or was there a deeper, more significant meaning? Rowan couldn't forget the way his eyes had met and held hers, as though trying to convey some more personal message, but she was none the wiser. Whatever else he was, Nathan Pride was both a disturbing and a confusing man. Rowan knew she was drawn to him, but her attraction was unwilling. His male chauvinism seemed to be deeply ingrained, and that, coupled with the conservatism of the medical profession, meant that he was a man who liked women to stay in their place. He had made no secret of this, and everything she had learnt about him confirmed it. And deep down Rowan knew she couldn't cope with that attitude on a permanent basis. In any relationship she had she needed to be an equal partner. She was too intelligent, too independent, too curious to find out things for herself for it to be any other way. The best thing to do with Nathan Pride was to keep him at a distance.

Her good intentions looked like floundering at the first test. Once again she and Nathan were in his car on their way to do a family interview. This time it was to see Dougal MacLaren and his aunt Elizabeth. Rowan had high hopes of being able to get his family involved, given their extensive pedigree with a number of diagnosed patients through two generations, but the fact that most of them were in the Western Isles might prove to be an insuperable problem.

Her other problem was that since their meal together several nights ago Nathan hadn't contacted her, and was, at the moment, acting the doctor rather than like a man who wanted to get to know her better.

The interview was going well. Elizabeth MacLaren made more of a fuss than was strictly necessary about giving the blood sample, but apologised profusely afterwards, clearly embarrassed by her anxiety over what she knew was a trivial procedure.

'It's just that I'm a coward over things like that,' she explained apologetically.

Rowan watched stony-faced as the fabled Pride charm was switched on and Nathan set out to put Elizabeth MacLaren at her ease and persuade her to act as a go-between with the rest of the family.

It was the first time Rowan had met Dougal's aunt, although she had heard a lot about her. The woman impressed her with her calm, caring attitude towards her nephew and her no-nonsense approach to his illness. The description she gave of the rest of the family was, however, one of utter disorganisation. Rowan didn't see how they were possibly going to be able to deal with them all at such a distance. Miss MacLaren said she would do what she could, and even Dougal said he'd talk to the family. And it was Dougal who remembered that there had been talk of an aunt on his mother's side being 'shut away' somewhere. Since all the other contacts were on his father's side of the family this was an interesting revelation.

His aunt showed no real surprise or concern at this piece of news.

'Och, aye, the MacPhersons have aye been daft,'

was her only pronouncement, sounding more like a Highland wifey than the teacher she now was.

'I think we'll run into some problems there,' Nathan prophesied as they drove home.

'Maybe the GP will be able to round them all up,' Rowan suggested hopefully, knowing full well that it wouldn't be a priority for a busy island doctor. 'You'll have to persuade him how important it is.'

Nathan merely grunted at that, the frown between his brows clearing as he thought the problem through. 'Maybe. But it would probably be easier to go up and do it ourselves. How about it, Rowan? A weekend away in the Western Isles collecting blood samples?'

The amusement running through his voice confused Rowan. Was he joking, or did he mean it about the trip, but was indicating that it would be more work than fun and she shouldn't read anything more personal into his suggestion? But, even so, a weekend away with him. . .

'It would be a more novel reason for a trip than bird-watching, certainly,' she agreed, deciding to be non-committal until she was more sure of Nathan's intentions.

To her disappointment this meant that he dropped the subject altogether, but then cheated her by suggesting they go for a drink.

'I've got a paper to finish when I get home,' he told her almost offhandedly, 'otherwise I would have offered you dinner.'

'That's perfectly all right,' Rowan was stung to retort, 'I've got work to finish too.'

Something in her tone must have jarred with Nathan as he shot her a quick, searching glance, but he said nothing.

Rowan regretted agreeing to the drink, feeling that

the invitation had been flung at her much like a bone to a hungry dog. It would have been wiser to make an excuse and go home. Conversation was stilted and Rowan, shifting uneasily in her seat, wondered how this almost unapproachable stranger could be the same man who had charmed her so convincingly a few days before.

Nathan, too, appeared to recognise the barrier that lay between them and took the blame for it.

'Sorry, Rowan. I've a lot on my mind at the moment, and I'm not very good company. I'll take you home.'

'You went out with Dad again, didn't you?'

They were having lunch in a café near the university. It had set out tables and chairs under big umbrellas to take full advantage of the hot summer weather. Summer tended to be a bit hit-and-miss in Glasgow, with a mixture of odd hot days and more that were cool or wet. Early summer was often the best weather, but everyone was making the most of these hot August days with memories of the Auld Alliance as cafés pretended they were in Paris rather than Glasgow. Matthew's question took Rowan by surprise, as she had expected him to have taken her earlier comments to heart and to leave the subject alone.

'It's none of your business,' she told him sharply, then felt mean was his young face fell. Determined as she was not to get involved with Matthew in a conversation about his father, Rowan realised that her 'no comment' statement could be misinterpreted.

'It was in the nature of business,' she finished somewhat lamely.

'Oh, right.' Matthew didn't appear to be particularly perturbed by Rowan's admission, and she felt a sense of let-down. Chiding herself, she acknowledged a no-win situation. She would have been equally annoyed if Matthew had been either pleased or disappointed, so to be cross when he was indifferent was totally perverse.

To change the subject Rowan asked Matthew what his plans were for the weekend, to be told that lazing around enjoying the sun was the extent of his forward planning. It didn't sound very exciting for an eighteen-year-old, but neither did her plans when Matthew demanded to know them.

'I really must make a start on that article,' she informed him with less than enthusiasm, wrinkling her nose at the thought. 'I can't put it off any longer.'

'You should be out enjoying yourself.'

'Hmm.' The temptation to say, *So should you*, was great, and the words hung on her lips, but she resisted, worried that Matthew might see that as an invitation that they should do something together. She contented herself with saying, 'You can make sure all the relevant computer print-outs are together. You had some of it out the other day.'

'Will do,' said Matthew.

They chatted inconsequentially for a while, then Matthew stretched back contentedly in his chair, his strong young arms spread wide.

'I feel as though I've always lived here. I really enjoy it.'

'Don't you miss your mother?' The words had popped out before she could stop them, but Rowan wasn't altogether sorry. She might have vowed she wouldn't discuss Matthew's mother with him, but that didn't mean to say she wasn't curious.

Matthew never mentioned his mother and, despite the ups and downs of his relationship with his father, had never shown any sign of missing her. Rowan remembered the closed, shuttered look which had appeared on Matthew's face before at the mention of his mother working, for here it was again. At first she thought he wasn't going to answer her, then he flung himself forward to sit hunched over the table, looking despondent.

'Will you think I'm really awful if I say that not only haven't I missed her for a second, but that it's wonderful to get away from her?'

'Oh, Matthew!' Sorrow, pity and sympathy were mingled in her response as she gazed at the boy who suddenly looked years younger than eighteen. She felt sorry for him, of course she did, but also, unexpectedly, for his mother. How hurt she would be to know how competely she was being rejected by her only son. Her only child.

'She never wanted me, you know.'

'Matthew!' Sounding thoroughly shocked, Rowan put down her coffee-cup to stare at him. 'That can't be true.'

'It is. When she and Dad split up, Dad wanted me to live with him. She only wanted me with her to spite him. Dad said maybe it was all for the best and we should avoid a court case and that I could spend holidays with him, and so on.' The words were spilling out of him now, and, guilty as she felt at hearing about Nathan's marriage, there was no way Rowan was going to stop Matthew talking. He had obviously been bottling his feelings up for far too long. 'It was fine at first, but then we moved south, so I saw less of Dad. I guess we drifted apart.'

Rowan's soft heart went out to the young boy who so clearly felt he had been rejected by both parents.

Maybe a custody case wouldn't have been so bad as this total sense of displacement.

'When did you move south?' she asked. Rowan didn't care if Nathan found out they had been discussing his marriage. Matthew obviously had the need to talk to someone.

'Ten years ago, but they'd separated two years before that.' It was as though a wall had crumbled and the flood of his feelings and memories poured fourth. 'They should never have got married in the first place.'

'But if they loved each other——' Matthew's exclamation cut her off rudely.

'They got married because I was on the way, that's all! Mother's father insisted.'

'Maybe your father thought it was the honourable thing to do,' she suggested hopefully.

'That's what he says! They're entirely unsuited. Medicine has always been everything to Dad, and he never wanted to do anything other than psychiatry. Mum wanted him to give up medicine and go into her father's company.' He pulled a face indicating clearly what he felt about that. There was no doubt that he was very much on his father's side, despite the antagonism that often surfaced between them. 'Anything where he'd make a lot of money. She's always thought she married beneath herself.'

'She could have refused to marry him,' Rowan pointed out.

He shrugged and, just for a second, showed some understanding of his mother. 'Not if you knew my grandfather. There was to be no illegitimacy sullying the family name. He threatened to cut her off if she didn't marry Dad.' He paused in his story as though considering something for the first time. 'Actually my grandfather's more part of the problem than I'd thought. He doesn't believe women should work——'

Where's the problem there? Rowan thought to herself. Your father has some very feudal ideas on the same topic.

'—and Mum, to be fair to her, was brought up to do nothing but socialise and lounge about looking decorative. That's all *her* mother ever did. She's still totally undomesticated. Dad, on the other hand, expected her at least to be domesticated if she didn't go out to work. Anyway, to cut this long story short, she calls him a boring do-gooder who'll never amount to anything and he calls her an empty-headed social butterfly who'll never amount to anything. End of story.'

'Matthew, I'm so sorry. It must have been very difficult for you.' So intent was Rowan on Matthew's feelings that she didn't give any thought to what she had learnt about Nathan.

He shrugged again. 'You get used to it. I'd be lying if I pretended my sympathies lie anywhere but with Dad. You're right, of course—he married her because it was the right thing to do. He does his best, but Mum, I'm just a nuisance to her. Especially now when I'm going to university.'

'What's the problem with that?' Rowan was at a loss to understand.

'A son at university makes her sound so much older than a son at school. I haven't met her *friends* for years. I think she still tells them I'm ten.'

Rowan was relieved to see he sounded more amused than hurt by that, but was dismayed when he went on, 'I'll turn up one day and really embarrass her.'

'Matthew, you wouldn't!'

'Maybe not. But she can be spiteful, and still is to

Dad, when she gets the chance. Not that he's a paragon, but with him it's more a case of stupidity.'

'What?' That caught unawares. What was Matthew saying?

'I grant you that Mum was very beautiful when she was younger. To be honest, she's not bad now, for her age. I expect Dad fell for a pretty face and didn't think any further.'

Since that tended to sum up Rowan's view of men she was inclined to agree, even though she didn't like to think of Nathan as being that gullible.

'What gets me is that he's doing the same thing now,' Matthew went on. 'A string of sexy, empty-headed girlfriends. I should be thankful he's never married any of them. I guess it's his way of protecting himself. He thinks all women are manipulative and not to be trusted, so he surrounds himself with ones who aren't and then he can say, "I told you so." It means he doesn't have to get involved and he doesn't have to get hurt — again.'

Matthew leant back in his chair and smiled at Rowan, a smug, self-satisfied sort of smile which he quickly hid. I've been had, Rowan thought to herself. Matthew had wanted to explain to her about his father's girlfriends. She had said she didn't want to hear. But in his own, quiet, charming, boyish, totally *devious* fashion Matthew had found a way to tell her — and she had listened.

The early morning sun sent shafts of bright light into her cool bedroom, highlighting the blue and grey with a golden glow and waking Rowan from her restless sleep. Knowing she would never go back to sleep and would only lie brooding about Nathan, she saw no point in staying in bed when she could be up, doing something useful. And so it was that Rowan found herself perched at her kitchen counter with a cup of fragrant coffee going through her papers at seven o'clock on a Saturday morning. As she flicked through a frown creased her brow. Something was missing. She went through again more carefully. No, one of the print-outs was definitely not there. About to blame Matthew, she decided he wasn't totally to blame. She should have sorted the papers out for herself. Still, all was not lost. The janitor would be unlocking the department at eight o'clock. A walk first thing in the morning before it became too hot and humid would set her up for the day.

'Damn you, Matthew,' she muttered under her breath as she rummaged through computer print-outs. 'What have you done with it?' The missing papers weren't to be found. Tempting as it was to phone him straight away in the hopes of getting him out of bed, the thought of getting Nathan on the phone instead was enough to make her wait until a more prudent hour.

'I'm really sorry, I've got it here, muddled up with some papers I brought home.'

Matthew didn't sound quite as sorry as Rowan thought he should, given the inconvenience he was putting her to, her foot tapping with impatience as he had gone to search his bag. And what papers could he possibly want at home over the weekend? she asked herself, and got no sensible reply.

'I'll bring them over to you, shall I?' Matthew was enquiring. 'When do you need them?'

'Now!' When did he think she needed them? Wasn't the fact that she had phoned him indication enough that she was planning to work on them that morning?

'OK. Give me time to dress and have some breakfast and I'll be over.'

Rowan sighed. It was ten o'clock. Surely he should be dressed by now? Seeing her whole morning disappear as she waited for Matthew to arrive when he felt like it, she made a quick decision.

'I'll be over to get them myself,' she told him firmly. 'Now.' And hung up before he could say anything.

Matthew tried to suppress a smug smile, but it broke through regardless. Concerned as he was about Rowan, he had decided that his plan was going so well he couldn't back out. Step three was about to start!

It said much for her preoccupation, and annoyance, that Rowan was halfway to the Pride residence when she realised that by doing this she might run into Nathan — immediately followed by the concern that he might think she was using this as an excuse to see him. It took all her resolve not to throw the car into an instant U-turn and return home.

CHAPTER SIX

As ROWAN pulled to a halt at the entrance to the drive she was presented with the rewarding view of long, tanned, muscular male legs in tight denim cut-offs, the top half of the body being buried somewhere inside the interior of Nathan's Volvo. At the same time she thought that this was someone intent on stealing Nathan's car, or at least its contents, was dismissed as she saw the paraphernalia of car-washing strewn around the gravel drive. The legs were certainly something, though Rowan again, eyeing them appreciatively as she resisted the desire to whistle, though through lack of ability rather than inclination, her feet crunching on the gravel as she approached. The legs had obviously heard the sound as the body started to withdraw.

'Matthew, what have you. . .?' The voice tailed off into silence as the figure emerged fully to take stock of who had been making the sound.

Rowan almost tripped over as she stopped as though shot, her widening gaze taking in the rest of the lean, muscular body that belonged to Nathan Pride. A body that had seen a lot of the sun recently, judging by its burnished bronze hue. Dumbfounded, Rowan could only gaze at the broad shoulders and deep chest, emphasised by the disreputable T-shirt, sleeves missing and which didn't quite meet the low-slung denim shorts, and showed a band of tanned skin between the two garments and an enviably flat stomach. By now Rowan's eyes had developed a will of their own and were sweeping down the strong legs to his bare feet, which were wearing nothing more than leather thong sandals.

He's gorgeous. The words rushed through Rowan's mind, demanding release, but fortunately her shock was such that speech was frozen along with all her other muscles. No amount of seeing Nathan, of thinking about Nathan, had prepared her for this. *Could* have prepared her for this. No matter how good Nathan had looked in his suits, nothing was going to prepare anyone to expect this tanned, muscled body beneath. Without his formal clothes, with his hair untidily flopping forward across his forehead, he looked more like Matthew's older brother than his father. More like a male pin-up, if she were to be really honest.

As her rocketing pulse steadied and breathing once more seemed a viable option, Rowan became aware that she was staring. Her physiology went haywire once more as blood rushed into her overheated face. Dragging her eyes up the length of his body to his face, she was disconcerted to see that Nathan looked nearly as embarrassed as she felt. But, even as she looked at him the tide of colour along his cheekbones receded and his mouth firmed into its habitual thin line. There was something oddly incongruous about the head of a consultant psychiatrist on the body of a beach boy. His very expression told Rowan that she was the last person he had expected to see.

'Rowan, you were quick!' Matthew hailed her from the door before either of them could speak, possibly saving them both from saying the wrong thing.

'You were expecting Dr Stewart?' By rights Matthew should have turned to a block of ice as the arctic chill of his father's voice cut through the warm summer air to reach him.

'Not so quickly.' Matthew shrugged as if to ask, Does it matter? and Rowan wondered what he was playing at. He had known she was coming over straight away, and she hadn't hurried, so there was nothing 'so quick' about her arrival at all.

'She's come to pick up a print-out I brought home with me by mistake.' Matthew nonchalantly offered the explanation to his father, whose rigid body was indicative of the anger he held in check.

'I see.' Something in Nathan's tone told Rowan that he saw very much more than she did. Whatever game Matthew was playing, his father obviously thought he had the measure of it.

Which is more than I do, Rowan pondered, as life slowly returned to her frozen limbs and she found she was able to hurry towards Matthew. To reach him she had to pass close to Nathan, and since he didn't make any attempt to move out of her path she had to swerve abruptly so as not to brush against him. But it wasn't fast enough to block out the intimate smell of his sun-warmed skin mingling with the musky fragrance of his aftershave. It was enough to have her stumbling on the gravel path, and she would have blundered into the brightly blooming border flower-bed if he hadn't caught her by the arm and steadied her.

His touch seared her flesh as his hand came into contact with her bare arm. Without conscious thought she shook his hand away and almost ran towards Matthew, who was still waiting by the front door.

'Come and have a coffee,' he invited. 'Or something long and cool. You look a bit hot and bothered.'

'I'll swing for you one of these days,' Rowan muttered under her breath, out of Nathan's hearing, and had to forcibly prevent herself from grinding her teeth at the guilelessly innocent smile he gave her.

'Want a drink, Dad?' he called over her shoulder to the man now collecting the car-washing gear together.

'Why not?' floated back the unexpected reply.

What game was Nathan playing? a very confused Rowan wondered. She would have bet anything that the last thing Nathan wanted to do was have coffee with her.

Matthew went straight to the kettle, leaving his father to pull out a chair at the kitchen table and invite Rowan to be seated. He leant negligently against the counter, his long legs crossed at the ankles, the pose somehow contriving to look both casual and attention-getting. Conscious that she was submitting to the need to stare, Rowan dragged her eyes away from the impressive picture he made to concentrate her attention on Matthew.

Putting three mugs of instant coffee on the table, Matthew pushed a black one towards Rowan but made no move to give his father's to him. Pushing himself away from the counter, Nathan sauntered over to the table and stood by another chair. He gave it, then Matthew, a long, piercing look before pulling it out and slowly lowering his body down to it. Matthew's chuckle was promptly stifled and even Rowan was forced to exert strict control over her facial muscles.

Nathan clearly intended to rise above the embarrassment of his too tight shorts which were making sitting a difficult and quite probably painful operation. That she should be the one blushing was unfair, in Rowan's opinion, but she couldn't help it as Nathan turned to her, amusement in the depths of his dark eyes.

'As must be obvious, these clothes aren't mine, but Matthew's, and although I can stand and bend in them

PRIDE'S FALL

I think sitting is going to prove beyond my powers of stoicism. The reason I'm wearing them,' he went on blandly when Rowan didn't so much as bat an eyelid, 'is a long story I won't go into now, but involves a challenge on Matthew's part which I rather stupidly took up. He's looking pleased with himself now——' and he was, Rowan noted, as she spared him a lightning glance '—because he thinks he's won a bet. What he doesn't know is that I've just changed the rules.'

Matthew banged his coffee-mug down on the table, but surprised Rowan once again by not saying anything. Why did she have the feeling that deep down Matthew was pleased about something? If Nathan's looks were out of character this morning so was Matthew's behaviour.

'I think I'd be better off standing,' Nathan essayed, easing himself to his feet as Rowan swallowed a gulp of too hot coffee, her mind blank as to a suitable response.

As he lounged once again against one of the kitchen counters, it was hard for Rowan to ignore his masculine beauty, even if she wanted to. Which of course she thought she should, but was honest enough to admit to herself that she didn't. The thought crept into her mind that maybe somehow Matthew had conned his father into wearing the shorts and T-shirt when he knew she was coming over in the hope of embarrassing Nathan. It seemed unlikely, and he would have had to work very fast, yet the idea persisted. It would explain the smug look that seemed to have settled permanently on Matthew as she checked him out again.

Rowan's eyes were drawn back to Nathan. If it *had* been Matthew's plan to disconcert his father he had come unstuck. Beyond his initial reaction, which

Rowan thought smacked more of anger than embarrassment, Nathan almost seemed to be enjoying himself. Just look at the way he was displaying his body now. And if comparisons were to be made — her eyes darting back to Matthew — there was no question of who came out the winner.

'If you could get the print-out for me I'd better be going,' she told Matthew, only then noticing her still almost full mug of coffee.

'There's no rush, is there?' Nathan asked conversationally, looking pointedly at the coffee, while Matthew made no move to fetch the offending papers. 'Maybe you'd rather have a cool drink?' he persisted.

'I don't want to hold you back,' Rowan protested, realising too late that it would have been safer to claim another appointment — a point borne out by Nathan's lazy insistence.

'You're not — washing the car will keep. And I've a feeling Matthew will be volunteering to do it.'

She looked imploringly at Matthew for help, but all she received from that quarter was a bland, 'Don't hurry on my account. I told you I had nothing planned.'

Silence stretched, and Rowan felt it encumbent upon her to make some kind of conversational gesture. Saying the first thing that came into her head, she wished she hadn't bothered.

'You've got a great tan.' The comment could only have been addressed to Nathan, who was several shades darker than Matthew, and, anyway, her eyes were once again fixed on his legs.

Matthew laughed, and the slight expression of discomfiture that crossed Nathan's face made her realise that he wasn't quite as blasé as she had supposed. Pleased to have dented his composure, she allowed herself to relax slightly, the knot of tension between her shoulders easing a little.

'It's the hours he spends pottering in the garden,' Matthew explained, making his father sound as if he was in his dotage. But there was no doubt in Rowan's mind that pottering wasn't the operative word.

'I didn't know you were a gardener,' she said, giving vent to her surprise, only to feel totally humiliated by Nathan's reply.

'Why should you?'

Sensing the tension mounting again, Matthew intervened. 'You could do with a bit more colour, Rowan; you're very pale,' he told her with more honesty than tact, but Rowan wasn't bothered by his observation.

'I'm too pale to tan really well, and I have too much respect for my health to spend hours lying in the sun.' Turning to Nathan, she asked challengingly, 'Don't you worry about skin cancer?'

He shrugged. 'Actually I'm quite careful. I just happen to have the type of skin that tans quickly. And darkly. And a lot of it's the result of the wind. Sailing,' he added, at her uncomprehending look. His smile was a flash of white in his now swarthy face, and in the disreputable clothes Rowan had the sudden image of him at the prow of a boat, face lifted to the elements. And not just any old boat, but an old-fashioned galleon in full sail, a bright scarf wrapped round his head and a gold hoop shining in one ear. Who would have thought that the suave Dr Pride would turn out to be so much like a wild, seafaring pirate? Her imagination took flight as she envisaged the strange, compelling picture of a piratical Nathan swinging her up in his arms and carrying her to his ship, kidnapping her as he set sail for far-away lands.

'Rowan?' The questioning tone told her she had

missed what Matthew had just said but that he was expecting some kind of answer. Blinking rapidly to dispel the last traces of the vivid images conjured up by her wayward imagination, she could only stare blankly at him.

'I imagine Rowan has better things to do with her time than spend them entertaining you.' It was back to Rowan, was it? She would have loved to know why he chopped and changed—sometimes 'Dr Stewart' and then disarming her with a friendly 'Rowan'.

'Surely you've time to finish your coffee. Or, better still, something long and cold while you relax for ten minutes in the garden. You can sit in the shade under the trees if you want to protect your skin.' Matthew repeated his invitation, twinkling brown eyes daring her to accept—or maybe he was daring her to go.

The slight frown crossing Nathan's face, instantly vanquished, was enough to decide her.

'I'd love something long and cool.' She met Matthew's gaze unflinchingly, and that young man, totally unabashed, winked at her, out of sight of his father's regard.

'Why don't you go into the garden and I'll bring some drinks out?' Matthew suggested, and Rowan didn't need a second invitation to escape the confines of the kitchen, which Nathan's overpowering presence made smaller than it really was. And exploring the garden was something she had been itching to do ever since she had discovered how much time Nathan spent there. It might give her more clues about him.

There was a wicker table and chairs at the bottom of the lawn, shaded by a couple of large fruit trees. She headed straight for them, and it was only as Rowan reached them that she saw the hammock slung between the trees. An instinctive exclamation escaped her lips as she stopped abruptly, causing Nathan, who she hadn't realised was so close behind her, to bump gently into her.

'What's the matter?' The urgency of his tone as he steadied her confused her, but she didn't have time to dwell on its meaning as his warm, dry hand gripped her bare arm for the second time that morning, the contact sending a fire flaming through her that had nothing to do with the heat of the sun.

'Are you all right?' he asked again, and it dawned on Rowan that her exclamation and sudden halt needed explaining.

'The hammock——' She pointed to it. 'It was a surprise.' As she turned her head to face him she found her face only inches from his, could feel his breath softly fanning her cheek. Mesmerised, she didn't move, and it was left to Nathan to drop her arm with a suddenness that suggested he had only just realised he was still holding it and move back from her, putting a safe distance between them.

'Ah!' A broad grin slashed his otherwise austere face, and he moved back towards her. 'Have you ever been in one?'

'No.' She eyed it warily, torn between the romantic image of lying back, a cool drink in one hand, the other trailing languidly over the side, and the more prosaic worry that it didn't look all that safe.

'You've missed something special,' Nathan informed her. 'It's the best way of lazily enjoying a rest on a hot summer's day. You must try it.'

'I couldn't——'

She was interrupted by a cheerful call from Matthew, crossing the lawn with a tray of three frosted glasses and a plate of biscuits. He set them down on the wicker table and eyed Rowan and his father, who were still standing. 'Have a seat, Rowan,' he invited. 'I'll get another chair.'

'No need,' Nathan said easily. 'Rowan's going to try out the hammock.'

'I don't think——' Again Matthew cut her off.

'Good idea. You'll enjoy it.'

Approaching it warily, Rowan realised that although it wasn't all that high there was no easy way to climb into it, and despite her full-skirted sun-dress she wasn't going to maintain any dignity or much modesty if she tried.

'No, really. . .' She backed away from the source of her problem straight into the waiting arms of Nathan. Before she knew what was happening one arm fastened round her shoulders, the other had slipped underneath her knees and she was being swept through the air, rather too close to a muscled masculine body for total equanimity, to be safely deposited in the rope bed.

'Oh!' was the most sensible response she could make in the circumstances when she had recovered her breath and her wits. And then, 'Oh!' again as Nathan settled a couple of cushions comfortably behind her head.

'Your drink, my lady!' Matthew was proffering the frosted glass, clinking with ice cubes, a knowing grin on his face at her heightened colour.

'Thank you.' Her grab for the glass was too quick and uncoordinated for the delicate balance needed to maintain comfort in the hammock, and it swayed dramatically.

Nathan was at her side immediately, steadying the unstable contraption and laying a restraining hand soothingly on Rowan's shoulder. 'Gently now,' he instructed on a laugh; 'we don't want you falling out.'

His eyes were warmly amused, but Rowan got the feeling he was inviting her to join in the laughter rather than laughing at her. 'Think of the teasing you'd get if you had to go to Casualty with a broken bone or dislocated joint because you'd fallen out of a hammock!'

The teasing *he'd* get — that was what he really meant, Rowan thought, disappointed as she took in his meaning.

'I'll be careful,' she promised, looking away, forcing her voice to sound neutral. 'Now I'd love that drink.'

She thought Nathan gave her an odd look as Matthew moved between them to put the glass carefully in her hand this time, but whatever he was thinking was quickly replaced by a blandly uncommunicative expression.

By dint of careful manoeuvring Rowan finished her drink, then relinquished the glass to a grinning Matthew. What's the matter with him now? She wondered crossly, then realised with a sinking heart that getting out of the hammock was going to be nearly as difficult as getting in. She was comtemplating her predicament and wondering if she could sort of half gracefully fall out when she glimpsed Nathan's face. He was grinning as broadly as Matthew. That the two men were united in enjoying themselves at her expense was enough to discomfit her further. Well, she would show them! She was just trying an experimental swing when she caught Nathan's eye.

'Don't even think it,' he told her firmly. Time seemed to slow down as Nathan's progress towards her took on the unreality of a dream sequence. It was as though he was gliding across the grass towards her, his movements unaccountably slowed by some strange force. 'If you want to get out I'll help you.'

It was still with an air of unreality that Rowan felt his arms close round her body as he braced himself to lift her. It was less helping her than doing it for her, she thought, as her arms slid round his neck and shoulders in what felt like a well-practised movement, and as he lifted her out of the hammock she pressed close to him, breathing in the now familiar scent of his warm male skin. Since she expected Nathan to put her down immediately he had her free of the hammock, it was with consternation that she realised he intended to do nothing of the sort. He was still holding her. And not just holding her—walking across the lawn with her in his arms, heading towards the house.

The kitchen was unnaturally dark after the bright sunlight, and Rowan blinked rapidly, trying to accustom herself to the gloom. Nathan's face, so close to her own, was nothing more than a dark blur. She wasn't sure how, when she had only intended to ask him to put her down, she found herself breathing his name. As her lips parted over the sound his head came down towards hers and, despite the gloom, his lips found hers with unerring accuracy. Although she wouldn't be able to remember the incident without embarrassment, at the time it seemed the most natural thing in the world to tighten her hold on him and go with the feelings that were flooding through her. As the kiss deepened Nathan slowly allowed his hold on her to slacken so that her legs slid downwards until she was balanced on her feet, her body still supported by his as his arms bound her to him.

The heat of his skin reached her through the thin T-shirt he wore, and as his body moved against hers she found her legs trapped by his, the awareness of the warm, naked thighs a tangible thing. A low moan reached her ears, but she couldn't have said which one of them was responsible for the noise.

As a sound, however, it galvanised her into action, and she pushed Nathan away, hastily stepping back from him, all the while noting with something like disappointment that he put up no struggle to hold on to her. She waited for him to make some trite comment, or to make fun of her, but he said nothing. Even then Rowan couldn't decide whether that was a good thing or a bad sign.

A clatter of sound from outside none too subtly announced Matthew's arrival. Rowan's cheeks grew hot as she wondered what Matthew had guessed from his father's behaviour to make him feel he needed to announce his imminent presence quite so loudly. Something in the gesture reminded her of what he had said about his father's girlfriends and left her with the feeling that she had been rather silly to get quite so carried away by what Nathan had probably only meant as a friendly salute.

Matthew pushed the door open and entered the kitchen with the tray of empty glasses, blinking against the dimness as he did so. Rowan's eyes, now adjusted to the level of light, didn't miss the grin that he was having trouble suppressing.

'Thank you——' she started to say.

'The pleasure was mine,' Nathan drawled, causing her to catch her breath and finish her sentence hurriedly.

'—for the drink.' She winced inwardly as she heard her voice cracking on the words. 'I'll get back to my work now.' She had just made an almighty fool of herself and all she wanted now was to get out of his sight and get home where she could dwell on her stupidity in private. If not quite an unprincipled rake,

Nathan was, nevertheless, a man who used women for his own ends. A man who made it plain he had no time for a permanent relationship in his life. A man who judged women by their decorative qualities only and expected them to stay in the background. Even his own son had been at pains to spell this out to her. So how come she, a sensible, intelligent woman, had quite unexpectedly, and against her better judgement, fallen in love with him?

'Rowan?' Once again Matthew had obviously asked her something, and she had no idea what. She looked at him blankly. 'Have you got everything?' he reiterated, and she nodded.

CHAPTER SEVEN

MONDAY morning had brought a change in the weather, and that, coupled with a brief glimpse of Nathan at a distance, resplendent in his dark grey suit and with Mike Knight, now his senior registrar, in tow, had Rowan wondering if she had dreamed the whole sequence of events that had been Saturday morning. She had almost convinced herself it *had* been a dream when Matthew shattered that hope. He was standing by the window, looking at the heavy clouds darkening the afternoon sky.

'Shame the weather's changed,' he remarked. 'The sun presents so many more possibilities for entertainment.' It was the very innocence with which he spoke that confirmed for Rowan that Saturday had been no dream and that somehow Matthew had engineered the setting for the 'entertainment'. As yet she didn't know why, but she was becoming ever more convinced that Matthew was playing some game of his own. A game, furthermore, in which she was one of the main pieces.

'Do you know what Dr Pride has done?' Jenny was positively bubbling over with enthusiasm and excitement.

'What?' Rowan asked warily, her heart leaping like an acrobat between her throat and her stomach. What on earth could have got Jenny so excited?

'He's sorted out the money. It's all going to work out.' She was grinning broadly, clearly expecting Rowan to join her.

'What money?' Rowan knew she was preoccupied and her brain wasn't functioning one hundred per cent, but she simply couldn't understand what Jenny was so worked up about.

Giving her a look between bewilderment at her obtuseness and concern at the reason for it, Jenny patiently explained, 'The money for the paint, wallpaper and so on. We're to get to spend it, the patients choosing what they like. It's all set for Saturday morning.'

'Saturday?'

This time Jenny's eyes narrowed as she looked carefully at Rowan, taking in the pallor beneath the light tan, the dark circles under her eyes, the dullness of the eyes themselves.

'Rowan, what on earth has happened?' All thoughts of money and Nathan Pride vanished as Jenny's concern was immediate and genuine for the other woman.

With a supreme effort of will Rowan managed to summon up reserves of energy from somewhere, forcing herself to stand straighter and even manage a smile. Not a very broad smile, true, but better than nothing.

'Nothing.' She kept her tone light, proud that she could and of the control she was exercising. 'I'm tired, that's all. I've been working too hard and not sleeping properly.' That much at least was true, Rowan reflected. There was no need for anyone to know why she hadn't been sleeping well the last couple of nights. 'Now, what were you saying?'

'Dr Pride has agreed to a shopping trip to the DIY store on Saturday morning. I told him we'd both go as well.' Noting the slight hesitation on Rowan's part, and the frown gathering between her brows, Jenny added, 'It is all right, isn't it?'

'Yes, fine.' Rowan forced her smile back again. 'Sorry, Jenny, I'm not really with it this morning.'

'Hmm.' Jenny looked decidedly sceptical, but in view of the anxiety on Rowan's face held her tongue.

'You make all the arrangements with Dr Pride,' Rowan continued, 'and let me know where you want me to be and at what time.'

'Is anything the matter?' Iain MacNamara looked at Rowan, concern written all over his youthful face, his deep blue eyes fixed on her, his attention caught, for once, by something other than his brother.

'I'm fine, just a bit tired.' She smiled at him with genuine gratitude for his concern, at the same time making a mental note to take herself in hand. When relatives of patients started to worry about the health of the therapist it was a disturbing situation. Apart from anything else she knew that Iain needed the sessions with her to deal with his own feelings about his ill brother, and that he relied on her to bolster his strength. It wouldn't do for him to see her weakening.

'I wish I could stop him wandering off.' Rowan's problems forgotten, Iain returned to his own. 'He was brought back by the police again last week.' He grimaced, then shrugged his shoulders. 'Actually, they were OK about it. One of them recognised Danny from the time before, and they just put him in the squad car and brought him home. Last time they took him to the station and I had to go and get him.'

'What was he doing?' asked Rowan.

'Running into the road in front of cars. He nearly caused an accident.' They both sat in silence for a moment, visualising Danny fighting off his unseen adversaries, dodging into the busy traffic and not thinking anything of it.

'I see why they brought him home,' Rowan agreed, wondering whether to mention the incident to Anna and get Danny's medication changed. But then simply doping him up wasn't much of an answer.

'Someone might have been killed,' Iain reflected. 'He might have been killed.' His voice broke and the silence was heavy with things unsaid. 'Sometimes I wonder if he wouldn't be better off dead,' he admitted, his voice so low that Rowan could barely catch his words, as he hung his head, not able to look at her while he said such things about his brother. 'After all, what has he got to look forward to?' He stopped and thought for a moment. 'I know you've told us that not everyone with schizophrenia has problems forever, that his delusions could go and he could lead a more normal life, but he's been like this for over a year now and I can see no sign of improvement. What if he never improves? What if this is as good as it gets?' His voice broke on a sob, and Rowan's heart went out to him. She knew he wasn't just worried about his brother, but also about his own responsibility to him and the limitations that put on his life.

'I love Danny, he's my brother, but I don't know that I can look after him forever.' The words were finally said, and, distressed as Iain was, Rowan could see that some of the burden had been lifted in merely speaking his thoughts aloud.

'You shouldn't have to,' she told him, hoping that she wasn't raising his hopes without some substance. 'Your parents——'

'——don't care.' The bitterness in Iain's voice told its own story and confirmed everything that Rowan already knew. The senior MacNamaras had washed their hands of their younger son and were only too glad Iain had picked up the responsibility they had shed.

'It might, and I only mean *might,* be possible to get Danny into a sheltered home,' she told him. 'He'd still need support from you, but you wouldn't be living with him.'

The blinding smile Iain flashed her momentarily startled her. It transformed his rather heavy face, making him look absurdly young to be shouldering such family problems.

'That would be great. I could leave home too then, get a bed-sit somewhere——'

'You want to leave home?' Rowan wondered why she was surprised. What young man wanted to live with his parents?

'Aye—have done for ages. But I can't leave Danny and I can't take him with me. But if we can both leave. . . I could get somewhere near him. I'm not abandoning him, it's. . .'

'I know—you don't have to explain. But don't get your hopes up too high just yet. It's not going to happen for a while, if at all!' In all honesty Rowan knew she had to add the last proviso, but it was like drawing a curtain over the ray of hope shining from Iain's face.

There was a good case to be made for moving Danny into one of the sheltered places in the new core and cluster housing group being planned, Rowan realised. His condition wasn't improving, and was unlikely to improve while he stayed in a home where it was made quite clear to him that he was a nuisance, an embarrassment, and he wasn't wanted.

A clatter outside announced Danny's arrival, causing Rowan to caution Iain quickly, 'Not a word of this to anyone.'

'Aye, Doc, not a word.' With a broad wink he moved out into the corridor to throw a leather-clad arm round his brother's shoulders, a spring in his step which had been missing when he arrived. The two youths went off noisily down the corridor, aiming friendly punches at each other and the air around them, both, for once, looking as though they had managed to shed their worries.

As she drove to the hospital on Saturday morning Rowan's heart was thumping painfully in her chest, her colour veering between an unhealthy washed-out pallor and an unbecoming fiery red. On balance she would rather have the pallor, she reflected, but every time she thought of Nathan the blood flooded into her face and she went hot with embarrassment. She hadn't seen him or heard from him. Ever one to be awkward, Matthew hadn't mentioned him. Several times it had been on the tip of her tongue to ask him something, anything, about his father, but each time she managed to restrain herself. The last thing she needed to do was give Matthew any idea she was interested in his father. Particularly after the warning he had given her.

Parking her car tidily by the entrance to the ward, she noticed Nathan's Volvo parked slightly to the side, in the shade. Rowan looked up into the cloudless blue sky. It could have at least rained, she thought briefly. The sun was too reminiscent of cold drinks, bare skin and hammocks.

The seven women, Jenny and Nathan all turned to look at her as she dashed in, and she was able to cover the rush of colour to her cheeks by glancing quickly at her watch as she hurried over to them.

'Sorry. Am I late?' Her watch told her she wasn't, but it seemed that everyone was eager to get on with the shopping trip.

The women had dressed up for the occasion, judging the shopping expedition to be an outing of some importance. Either that, or Nathan's presence on his day off had something to do with neatly combed hair and lipsticked mouths — even if, in Pat's case, neatly combed meant a series of lethal-looking spikes and her lipstick was a whiter shade of pink. For all that the black shading her eyes made her look as though she hadn't slept for a month, there was something naïvely attractive about her. With something like a start Rowan realised that underneath the girl's outlandish appearance and habitually sullen expression she was very pretty — something Nathan appeared to have noticed, judging by the way he was smiling down at her when she spoke to him.

She's a patient, Rowan wanted to snap at him, behave yourself! when she realised it was her own jealousy talking. There was nothing improper in Nathan's manner or the friendly smile he was giving Pat — exactly the same smile he was bestowing on Maggie and the other woman. A smile that froze slightly, slipping from his eyes, tightening his lips, as his gaze came back to Rowan.

He was wearing a stone-coloured knitted cotton sweater, its loose shape hinting at the muscled body beneath, and casual trousers in a slightly darker shade. The fact that he looked less like a doctor encouraged the women to treat him less like one. It seemed informality was to be the order of the day. Even Jenny seemed to be more relaxed with him. Rowan was glad she had put on a brightly coloured cotton skirt and top with some chunky wooden jewellery. It was casual, but also acknowledged that for the women this was a special occasion. Nathan had had nothing to do with her choice, she insisted to herself. She pulled her attention back to the conversation to realise that a wrangle had broken out over who was to go in which car.

Ushering them out into the courtyard, Nathan announced that he would take three of the women and they could swap coming back. Pat was in his front seat before anyone else moved, and Rowan noticed Maggie making determinedly for his car too, followed by another woman. Jenny led two others to her car.

'Come with me.' Rowan smiled at Jean and Betty, opening her car doors for them. 'Who wants to sit where?'

'Can I sit in the back?' Jean asked rather nervously. 'I don't like cars very much. I'm not used to them, I suppose.'

'Of course you can.' Rowan helped her in. 'How do you feel? Do you want to go through with this?'

'Oh, aye.' Jean smiled bravely through her nerves. 'I'm looking forward to seeing the shops — I've never been to one of those big stores. Seen the adverts on the telly, though. It's just the car that worries me a bit.'

Betty turned from her front seat to smile at her. 'You'll be fine. If you panic, grab me, though, not the doctor. Not while she's driving.'

For a moment Rowan thought that dire warning was going to precipitate a panic attack, but Jean seemed to get a hold on herself and nodded at the other two.

'I'll remember.'

Rowan turned on the ignition and put the car into gear, watching Jean in the rear-view mirror as she did so. She paled slightly but looked up, and catching Rowan's eyes on her, gave a shaky smile. She's got more guts than we've been giving her credit for,

Rowan marvelled, and wondered what other challenges Jean had faced silently alone.

As she drove along Rowan also reflected on how easy it was, even with the best will in the world, to misjudge patients and their experiences. She and Jenny had realised that none of the women had been to one of the big DIY warehouses before, and Jenny had taken the time to explain to them what it would be like. Neither of them, however, had stopped to think that riding in a car was also a novelty for these women. She wondered if Nathan had thought of it.

'It's going to be a nightmare,' Jenny had told Rowan, showing her the list for the wallpaper and paint. She had a very organised plan showing room sizes, amount of materials needed and who belonged in which room, and with whom. 'This is only for the bedrooms,' she pointed out. 'We'll have to sort out the other rooms later.' She sighed deeply. 'We should also have taken them a couple at a time.'

In the event, it was very much less of a nightmare than the two women had envisaged—due, it had to be said, in large part to Nathan. Whether he was behaving like a doctor or just like a man was a moot point, but he quite simply took charge, and the women fell in with his plans, going off to inspect the wallpapers and paint charts. Rowan thought the size of the place, busy with weekend shoppers, might have been a problem, but Nathan made sure the women knew how to recognise the staff by their uniforms and told them exactly where to wait if they got lost. Everything seemed to be in hand.

She noticed one or two people looking at the women oddly and move hurriedly out of their way. It pained Rowan to admit it, but, despite their best efforts, the women still didn't look quite —— She cut the thought off before it could form. She refused to say 'normal' or even 'right'. They had a style that was all their own. It was just a pity it had to say 'psychiatric patient' to everyone in the vicinity. In fact the only one who didn't draw stares was Pat, with her spiky hair, unrelieved black clothes and exotic make-up.

The two pairs of women who would be sharing rooms were the ones Jenny was most concerned about, since they had to agree. There was no trouble between Betty and Jean, who quickly agreed on a very pretty pale floral paper, predominantly greens and peaches on a creamy background. Rowan was amused to note that Betty picked out a fairly bright peach paint to go with it, and was firmly dissuaded by Jean, who steered her towards a lovely clotted-cream colour. There was definitely more to Jean than met the eye, and Rowan left them planning a pale green carpet.

The other pair were more of a problem. Nan picked out a paper in a lurid purple with turquoise splodges which Rowan supposed were intended to represent flowers. She couldn't begin to imagine why such a paper had ever been produced, so ugly it seemed. She could quite understand why Dora was refusing to contemplate it, insisting that it would bring on a relapse. Rowan agreed. It would bring on a relapse in anyone — or at the very least a migraine. Cravenly leaving Jenny to adjudicate, she went in search of the others.

Maggie, true to form, had her pink paint, a soft pinky coral, and wallpaper in several corally tones on a hazy shell-pink background. It promised to be both pretty and sophisticated. Looking at the middle-aged woman in her washed-out cotton print dress and baggy cardigan, Rowan felt a lump in her throat. How much more ability these women have than we ever give them a chance to use, she thought, as she looked round to see how Pat was getting on.

The girl was nowhere in sight, and with a mounting sense of alarm Rowan set off to look for her. She rounded one of the stacks of shelves to see Pat at the other end of the aisle, apparently deep in conversation with a youth who, judging from his dress, worked in the store. Even from this distance Rowan could see the tension in Pat's body and realised the encounter was not of the girl's choosing. As she watched the youth leant towards Pat, one arm coming out to rest against the shelves, effectively blocking her path. Before she could move to her rescue Nathan loomed into sight, and summing up the situation with one brief glance gathered Pat up and led her away from the young man, who seemed suddenly to have shrunk both in size and stature.

'OK?' Rowan heard him ask as the two of them walked towards her, and saw Pat nod, giving Nathan a look which clearly said, My hero!

She tried to tell herself that her concern was for Pat and not sour grapes on her part as she watched them. It wouldn't do Pat much good just at the moment to develop some sort of crush on Nathan. After all, it hadn't done *her* any good, had it?

'How are the decisions coming?' Rowan asked Pat, the three of them returning to the wallpaper section.

Pat shrugged offhandedly. 'I don't know. It's all a bit ordinary, isn't it?'

Rowan, having a moment's vision of the purple and turquoise effort, suppressed a shudder and gave thanks for the blandness of most of the styles.

'You've got a room of your own, haven't you?'

Nathan asked, although he knew the answer perfectly well.

'Yes.' Pat's face came alive with anticipation. 'Jean and Betty insisted. It's only a tiny room, but they said I should have it and they'd share. Jean said at my age I needed space to myself to put up posters and make a mess.' She grinned, looking younger than ever. 'She pretended to be horrified at the idea, but really she was being ever so kind. I'm really looking forward to living with them. It'll be like a family.' The happiness on her face at the idea moved Rowan, and as she caught Nathan's eye she realised that he was also touched by Pat's enthusiasm. When she forgot to be moody and tough Pat came across as a very nice young woman. Rowan hoped against hope that she would do well, that her one brief episode of illness would be no more than that.

'Jean and Betty have decided on this,' Rowan said, pointing to the appropriate paper on the shelf, and surprised a wistful look in Pat's eyes.

'Not surprised,' she muttered. 'Not very exciting, is it?'

'No, but pretty,' Rowan pointed out. 'And easy to live with. You don't really want something you'll get fed up with quickly, do you?'

'S'pose not,' Pat agreed half-heartedly.

'What about this?' Nathan picked up a roll of sombre cream and beige stripes and replaced it hastily at the glance the two women gave him. 'Only trying to help,' he told them, receiving a non-committal grunt from each of them.

His action united the two women, however, in pitting their taste against that of a mere man, and Rowan looked at him thoughtfully, sure that he had done it on purpose. She had been watching Pat carefully and come to some conclusions of her own. Now she picked up another paper.

'What about this?' she asked. 'Or this?' when Pat shook her head. 'I really like this one,' she added, picking up a third paper, a pretty floral one which she had noticed Pat's gaze kept returning to. She unrolled a length.

'It's a bit twee,' Pat muttered, but by now Rowan was sure this was the paper the girl wanted but for some reason was ashamed to say so.

'Very feminine,' Nathan put it. 'It suits you,' he added, smiling at Pat.

For the first time that Rowan could remember Pat blushed, a deep dark red, and turned her head away.

Glancing sharply at Nathan, Rowan was surprised to see the expression on his face. For a second she had wondered if he was flirting with the girl, no matter how unethical that would be. Now she realised it was something very different. He too had noticed Pat's reluctance to admit her preference in wallpaper and was doing something about it.

Eventually Pat turned back to the shelf and picked up the roll where Rowan had placed it, allowing a couple of feet to unroll. Cornflowers, poppies and golden corn were gathered into small bouquets and scattered across a white background. The colours were clear and bright, but there was nothing loud or brash about the paper.

'Do you really think it suits me?' Pat asked, carefully looking at Rowan rather than Nathan.

'Yes, I do,' she said gently but firmly.

'I wouldn't look silly with it?'

'Of course not. Why should you? It's bright and cheerful and pretty and, as Dr Pride says, feminine. It's you,' Rowan smiled encouragingly.

'I've always wanted something like this,' Pat confessed, putting the paper back on the shelf and staring at it. 'My room at home was always so dingy, and Mum said it wasn't worth doing up just for me. I used to dream of having a really pretty bedroom. I could now, couldn't I?' She looked at Rowan and Nathan and they could see the tears in her eyes. It seemed a breakthrough could come as well in a shop as a clinic.

'Yes, of course you can. As pretty as you like,' Rowan told her, her own eyes bright with unshed tears she was rapidly blinking back.

The next thing she knew Pat had flung herself at her and she was enveloped in a bear-hug as both women sniffed back tears and hugged in a moment of pure emotion while Nathan looked on. As they parted Rowan thought she heard him mutter, 'Women!' under his breath, sounding, for once, entirely male and not the slightest bit the psychiatrist. She knew, by Pat's grin, that she had heard him too.

'If that's the decision made I'll go and get the trolley and you can load up the paper,' he announced, his gruff tone belied by the smile he gave Pat. 'You enjoy your pretty room,' he told her, stretching out a hand towards her head. For an instant it was as though he was going to ruffle her hair, as he might a child's, but in the end he settled for gently patting her spikes. 'I've always wondered what they felt like,' he told the astonished girl, before swinging away to collect the trolley.

'Isn't he super?' Pat breathed in something like awe, once more raising Rowan's level of concern. She hoped Nathan knew what he was doing. 'I really wish I had a dad like him!'

It was all Rowan could do to stop her mouth falling open to thud on the floor. Here she had been worrying about Pat by attaching her own feelings for Nathan on to the girl, when all she was going through was a classic pattern of wish-fulfilment projected on to the nearest appropriate male. Yes, Pat was infatuated with Nathan, but as an idealised father figure; the father she had never had. And of course, Nathan knew and understood that, and would deal with it when the time came in his own professional way.

And it was Nathan who suggested the perfect end to the successful shopping trip.

'There's a very nice pub along the road,' they heard him telling the women in astonishment. 'A big garden with tables and umbrellas, just the thing for a day like this. What do you say?'

The answer was, of course, a foregone conclusion, and since Jenny and Rowan weren't consulted they found themselves sipping white-wine spritzers with the women while Nathan settled for a lager, all of them under brightly coloured umbrellas in a sunny pub garden.

It was Betty who felt the need for some kind of speech.

'We just want to say thank you,' she told them. 'It's been the best Saturday morning—best any morning, come to that—that any of us can remember in a long while.' Much head-nodding from the others accompanied her remarks, and Rowan found herself embarrassed that they should be so grateful for so little.

'It's been our pleasure,' Nathan replied with all his charm in evidence, 'and I'm sure I speak for the others when I say we look forward to being invited round for a cup of tea when you're settled in your new homes. A social visit rather than a professional one,' he added, receiving a barrage of nods and smiles.

The journey back to the hospital was accomplished

without fuss, and the ladies went off, only slightly late for their lunch. Jenny waved to the other two and rushed away, leaving Rowan and Nathan standing between their cars in the now deserted courtyard. Turning from him, Rowan reached her car and had her hand on the door-handle when Nathan's voice reached her.

'Rowan.'

CHAPTER EIGHT

ROWAN stopped in her tracks and let Nathan catch up with her, but she couldn't bring herself to turn and look at him. She didn't understand anything about Nathan these days, or where she stood with him. If Matthew was playing some sort of game with her, so was his father, and she felt as though she was caught between the two of them. The Pride men were becoming more trouble than they were worth.

'Are you in such a hurry?'

If he hadn't sounded so amused, so sure of himself and of her, Rowan's answer would have been very different. But his confidence galled her. She wasn't one of his girlfriends, to come running when he snapped his fingers. Rounding on him, her temper rising, she looked him straight in the yes, and lied; 'Actually, Nathan, I am.'

The words stopped him dead. 'Oh! I thought. . .' For the first time since she had met him Rowan was seeing Nathan Pride lost for words. It was a pleasing sensation. 'I was hoping. . .'

'If you wanted me for another family interview, Nathan, you should have mentioned it earlier. I *do* have other things to do.' Her sarcasm wasn't lost on him, and she was pleased to see his cheekbones tinge with pink.

'*Actually,*' he stressed her word with sarcasm of his own, 'I was hoping we could have driven out for a late lunch somewhere in the country, but since you're busy...' He let the words trail away. 'I'll see you soon, Rowan.'

And he left her, mourning the loss of the time she could have spent with him, but still resentful that he should assume she was always free when he felt like being with her.

Rowan leant against the rail of the Island ferry, enjoying the carefree feeling of the wind blowing through her hair and the warm sun beating down from a surprisingly clear blue sky. Even if she wasn't too sure how she came to be on her way to visit a family in the Islands with Nathan she was glad to be here, and determined to enjoy every minute.

'Do you know Mull?' he asked, coming up silently behind her, to drop a careless arm round her shoulders, drawing her close to his side.

Her heart turning over at his nearness and casual intimacy, she steadied her voice before replying.

'I've visited a couple of times, but I wouldn't count that as knowing it.' She looked up, and found herself caught in a hypnotic stare that seemed set to render her speechless.

'I came here quite a bit when I was younger,' he informed her, 'but I haven't been for ages.'

'Is that why we've come?' she asked. There was a nagging question at the back of her mind about the trip.

'We've come to interview the MacPhersons,' he reminded her, a smile tugging at the corner of his lips. 'You know that.'

'Yes.' Her reply was hesitant. 'But why them?' This was the nub of the matter. 'They didn't seem to be the most promising of the leads we've been given.'

'They're not,' Nathan confirmed instantly, 'but they do have a couple of points in their favour. Most particularly, they've agreed to be interviewed now, and they're all home.'

'Oh.' Rowan dragged her eyes away from his and forced them to focus on the craggy outline of Duart Castle, perched on its cliff-top as the ferry forged its way past.

'I know some of the other islands have more interesting leads, but I thought we'd go there later,' Nathan told her.

'Ah.'

'And I thought a weekend away now would be nice.'

'Yes.' Her mind still reeling with the notion of other weekends away with Nathan, Rowan realised her conversational skills were sadly lacking, but Nathan didn't appear to mind.

'Is your room all right?' Nathan stood up as she came into the hotel's drawing-room, drawing her down beside him on a large, comfortable, old-fashioned sofa.

'Beautiful,' she told him, 'and the views up the Sound are breathtaking.'

He smiled a satisfied smile at her. 'I thought you'd like it.'

Like it? She loved it!

'After all the work you've done on the project I thought you deserved a perk,' he added.

An eyebrow arched as she looked at him, but he forestalled her hasty speech.

'All expenses on the project, and no arguing.'

Rowan took a deep breath to say, 'Absolutely not,' and to her astonishment heard herself meekly agreeing with him. She knew that Nathan wouldn't, and couldn't, put the cost of this trip on his research grant, but if he wanted to pay. . . . so be it.

* * * *

It was midsummer and the evenings were still long, so they opted for a walk before a late dinner. Driving up on the Friday afternoon meant they would have an unhurried Saturday interviewing and taking blood samples before heading back to Glasgow on Sunday. And two evenings to fill together, Rowan told herself happily.

The hills rose up around them, the majesty of Ben More in the background as they set off from the hotel towards the shore, their thoughts unspoken but their feet in agreement as to their destination.

'I should have worn my wellies,' Rowan mourned, as she skipped from rock to rock, narrowly missing a pool left by the outgoing tide. She glanced at her serviceable shoes which, while stout enough for walking, would not take her paddling. And one look at the still icy, rock-strewn water told her paddling without boots was out of the question—here, at least.

'We'll go to Dervaig Sunday morning,' Nathan offered. 'I've booked us on the last ferry. It's a shame we can't stay until Monday. . .' His voice trailed off as his eyes once again locked with Rowan's.

This is getting to be a habit, she thought in some confusion, a nice habit, but I'm not sure what it means. Nathan found his voice again. 'But I've an outpatient clinic first thing.'

Still entrapped in his warm gaze, Rowan stumbled and would have slipped into another pool if Nathan hadn't steadied her, grabbing then holding her firmly by the arm.

'Thank you.' For such a small stumble she sounded rather breathless, but if Nathan noticed he didn't comment, merely sliding his hand down her arm to capture her hand as he led her along the rocks. Even when they regained the gravelly shore he didn't release it, and Rowan was happy to simply walk hand in hand along the shoreline with him, stopping from time to time to examine pretty shells and interesting pebbles. Making for another rocky outcrop, they settled themselves to watch the sun go down. Lit with lilacs, pinks and purples, the sky was an artist's delight, and so beautiful that Rowan wouldn't have believed it unless she had been there to witness it. A slight breeze had sprung up, and she was glad of Nathan's warm bulk next to her. It was only as she snuggled into the warmth of his shoulder that she began to wonder if she was taking too much for granted. She might love Nathan, but she had no idea of his feelings for her. For once, however, they were in total accord as Nathan's arm wound round her shoulder and pulled her into the curve of his body so that she had no need to be concerned about being presumptuous.

'Rowan.' His breath tickled her ear and she sighed deeply, not wanting to move and break the magic of the moment and sure that Nathan was about to suggest their return to the hotel. She buried deeper into the comfort of his sweater, breathing in the scent of him which had haunted her since he had carried her to the hammock in his garden, only to hear him whisper, 'Rowan,' again.

Forcing herself to look at him, she discovered his head coming down to meet hers, and before she could fully take in what was happening his lips covered hers in a kiss to take her breath away.

This was a kiss unlike any they had shared before. This time Rowan knew that she loved him, and part of her wanted to keep that hidden from him, while another, more courageous part of her was winding her arms round his neck to hold him ever tighter, not wanting the kiss to end.

She had no idea how much later it was that Nathan slowly withdrew from her embrace. Even as she tried to hold on to him his hands were on hers, loosening their hold. It was only because she could see the genuine reluctance in his eyes to let her go that she could release him.

'We'd better be getting back.' His voice broke on the words as he leant forward to kiss her again, although the firm grip he kept on her hands prevented her from holding him to her.

'Do we have to?' Rowan was embarrassed by the almost pleading tone in her voice and the involuntarily spoken words. Her composure wasn't helped by the gleam in Nathan's eyes as he drew her to her feet. She still didn't altogether trust him, but her feelings were somewhat mollified by his admission.

'Yes, we do,' he asserted reluctantly, 'if only for my own sanity. You're altogether too tempting, Rowan Stewart.'

The MacPhersons might have agreed to be interviewed and give blood samples, but things weren't to be so straightforward when Rowan and Nathan arrived the next day. Two of the three men were out somewhere unspecified, and those of the family who were there eyed Nathan's syringe with grave disquiet. Deciding that the family history might be the best place to start, Rowan sat down with Mrs MacPherson to piece together the family tree. No easy task, as Shona MacPherson was apt to wander off into tall tales of her relatives. Eventually Rowan established that an aunt of Shona's had been sent to Lochgilphead, the psychiatric hospital on the mainland, and was, as far as she knew, still there. Slightly shocked at how easily Mrs MacPherson could dismiss her now elderly aunt,

Rowan put this out of her mind as she set to both draw out Shona MacPherson and keep her broadly on the subject.

Nathan had persuaded both Mrs MacPherson and her daughter to give blood samples, and everything was becoming a bit easier when Mr MacPherson and his brother Hector returned. Wherever they had been, it involved the drinking of alcohol, and it immediately became apparent that Hector had had more than was good for him. Or anyone else, come to that. Staring at Rowan, he sat down opposite her, his eyes following every move she made, his leering expression making her increasingly uncomfortable.

Donald, who had not had as much to drink as his brother, tried to persuade him into the other room, but Hector wasn't to be moved.

Nathan left Mrs MacPherson holding a piece of cotton wool to her arm where he had taken her blood and placed himself firmly between Rowan and her unwanted admirer. With Nathan's solid bulk between her and Hector, Rowan felt a little easier and gave him a quick grin of thanks. It wasn't to be that easy, though.

'Out of the way, Doc. Let's look at the lass you've brought us.' Hector's words were slurred, and although Rowan knew it was largely the alcohol talking it didn't really help her to feel any better. She wasn't sure whether Nathan had no intention of moving or whether it was that he didn't move fast enough for Hector. Whatever the reason, before she knew what was happening Hector was trying to push Nathan out of the way. Caught off guard, Nathan rocked on his feet, but stood his ground as Donald leapt to his feet to restrain his brother, while Mrs MacPherson flapped helpless hands and begged her brother-in-law to behave himself.

Noticing Nathan's hand clenching into a fist, Rowan caught at it, not wanting him to do something they'd all regret.

'It's OK, Nathan,' she urged him, while Donald showed his true mettle as he manhandled his larger brother out of the room.

He was back a moment later, full of apologies, but Nathan was still too angry to be easily placated. Rowan watched him wonderingly as he visibly struggled to keep his temper and remain polite, but was still astonished to hear him announce their departure. Before her startled wits could gather themselves to protest Nathan had bundled her out of the house, throwing a comment over his shoulder to the effect that he'd be back.

'There was no need for that. . .' Rowan began as Nathan forcibly dragged her to the car. 'I could —'

'Shut up!' She was so taken aback by his words and actions that to the surprise of both of them she did just that.

'Sorry. I shouldn't have taken it out on you,' Nathan apologised as they both sat in the car. 'Are you all right?' He turned to look at her, smoothing her silky hair away from her face as he gazed deep into her eyes. He kissed her fiercely. 'I seem to find it hard to be reasonable where you're concerned.'

Rowan hugged this thought to herself as they drove back to Glasgow on Sunday, her memory lingering on the fun they had had visiting Mull's Little Theatre, the kisses they had shared when they stopped on the starlit journey back to the hotel. There had been more kisses on the beach that morning, and Rowan knew that they had never been so close, never so at one with each other. But despite the closeness Nathan had not mentioned the future. She couldn't believe he didn't care for her but as they neared the city he was withdrawing from her. And she didn't understand why.

Anna was staring at her in complete amazement. 'You mean this has been going on all summer and I didn't know anything about it?'

Almost against her will and certainly against her better judgement Rowan had astounded herself by suddenly pouring out the whole story to her friend over what should have been a working lunch. Maybe it was because of Matthew reminding her that he stopped working for her at the end of the week. Maybe with the new term only a couple of weeks away it seemed as though the summer was over. Whatever it was, Rowan had found herself pouring out her confusion to Anna.

'*Nothing* has been going on all summer,' Rowan pointed out with some asperity. 'That's just the point.'

'And you're complaining about that?'

'No! Yes. Oh, I don't know. What does the man think he's doing?' Rowan's exasperation was showing, and she felt some relief at finally being able to give voice to it. She might love Nathan with all her heart, but her mind was telling her other things, among them that she was annoyed with him—very annoyed. This blowing-hot, blowing-cold behaviour simply wasn't fair. Since their weekend away they had been out a few times, but although Nathan had kissed her with a real depth of feeling their relationship was stagnating, not progressing. Now he was away again.

'If you ask me, he's running scared,' Anna offered

her opinion while making patterns with the chocolate on top of her cappuccino.

'I don't understand.' Rowan looked at her friend as though she were speaking her native Gaelic, which Anna had been known to do on occasion — usually after several glasses of wine.

'It's obvious Nathan's attracted to you, but you're not his usual sort of woman. He likes them beautiful and brainless, decorative and not much more.'

'Thanks. You're making me feel heaps better.' Rowan stared gloomily into her coffee.

'Don't be obtuse. You know what I mean. You're attractive, but not in that high-gloss, superficial way his women usually are. You're very bright, you've got a demanding job, and Nathan's not used to that. You employ his son. I bet he's as confused as you are.'

'Hmm. If I believe that I'll believe anything,' Rowan told her friend shortly. 'The man's a cheap opportunist who changed his mind.'

Anna didn't reply immediately, her brow furrowed as she concentrated on something that had just occurred to her. 'You know, now that I come to think of it, I don't remember seeing Nathan with any glamorous girlfriend in tow all summer.'

'Would you expect to?' Rowan was surprised Anna would expect to see Nathan at all.

'Yes. We often run into him at concerts. I saw him once with Matthew, in fact, but no woman. And he came to Bob Clarke's retirement do on his own. No there've been several occasions when I would have expected him to have some glamorous bit either with him, or coming to collect him, but not this summer. Not a sign.'

'It doesn't necessarily mean anything,' Rowan

insisted. 'Maybe he feels he needs to be more responsible now that Matthew's living with him.'

'Maybe,' Anna agreed, sounding thoroughly unconvinced.

'Will you have dinner with me tonight?' Matthew smiled winningly, and Rowan, although part of her mind told her she should object, knew she would give in. Now that his last day had come she acknowledged just how much she was going to miss Matthew — at least, she acknowledged it to herself. She didn't need to give him a swollen head by admitting it to him.

'Thank you very much; I'd love to.' Her smiling acceptance momentarily surprised Matthew, who, it seemed, had been expecting her to demand to know why or otherwise prevaricate.

'Great. I thought we had to celebrate——'

'You mean that you're finally leaving me?'

'No! That we got through the summer together. You must admit, at times it seemed a long shot.'

'Yes, well. . .' Rowan didn't want to talk about Nathan. She did her best not to think about him, but that seemed to be getting harder with each passing day. And her dreams were outside her control altogether.

'I'm going to miss you.' The words were hurriedly spoken before she said something else she might regret.

'Will you?' The idea seemed to cheer Matthew up, his smile brightening perceptibly.

'Of course. I've got used to having you around the place. And you've been surprisingly useful. I shall have to go back to running all my own errands now.'

'What about my charm, my wit, my good looks, my——?

'Can't say I'd noticed,' Rowan butted in, her tone as teasing as his. 'You make a great cup of coffee, though.' As she grinned at Matthew, attempting to lighten what was threatening to become an emotional moment, their eyes met, and before she realised quite what was happening Matthew had taken her in a great bear-hug, almost swinging her off her feet as he kissed her enthusiastically on the cheek.

'I know I started this job as a joke, but I've really enjoyed working here this summer. We won't lose touch, will we?'

'No, of course not. But you'll soon settle down and won't have time for me.'

'I'll always have time for you, Rowan — you know that.'

Rowan felt the same twinge of anxiety she had before at the intensity of Matthew's tone as once again she wondered if he had a crush on her. Most of the time she was sure he hadn't, but every now and then. . . She sighed. The Pride men certainly had complicated her life.

Life was slipping out of her control at an alarming rate. As she watched Nathan standing at the college club bar collecting their drinks Rowan pondered how she had come to be sitting there, waiting for him. They had bumped into one another and had somehow turned automatically towards the club. It had been Nathan who had broken the silence, but only to ask her what she wanted to drink.

Now he put the white wine in front of her and took the seat opposite, but said nothing. Racking her brain for something to say that was passably intelligent and non-controversial, Rowan found herself sadly bereft of ideas. It was with desperation that she launched into the only topic that presented itself.

'Was the conference good? I'm sure——'

'Dammit, Rowan, I didn't bring you here to talk about the conference!' The undertone of anger that ran through Nathan's voice startled her, and she glanced up to see his eyes firmly focused on her, their velvet brownness glittering with some pent-up emotion as a muscle throbbed beside his mouth, which was set in a tight, angry line.

Why was he so angry? Rowan couldn't think of one good reason why he should be looking at her as though she were the cause of immense problems in his life. If either of them had a right to be angry it should be her. He hadn't spoken to her in well over a week. Caught in his gaze like a trapped animal, she couldn't break away, her eyes under the control of his, and that annoyed her. She was annoyed with him, his anger, his arrogant manner, his proprietorial attitude, but she was also annoyed with herself for sitting there and meekly giving in to it, her knees weakening and her heart thumping in response to his dominant masculinity. The man's a menace, a tiny, rational part of her mind insisted. You're a fool to listen to him, to respond to him in this way. She did her best to listen to this voice, to let it fuel her own anger. She would need it if she was not to be overwhelmed by Nathan. Deciding to meet him halfway, she threw out a challenge.

'Why did you bring me here, Nathan?' she asked, her tone bordering on the insolent. That seemed to take him aback, for his eyes widened, then narrowed, before clearing as some of the anger left his face and he settled back in his chair, a half-smile twisting his lips, although not with real humour or kindness.

'Two reasons,' he told her smoothly, 'the main one

being to discuss your relationship with Matthew.' His lips stretched slightly into a wider smile, but there was still no warmth in it.

Something about his expression alarmed Rowan, and her skin prickled with apprehension as she gave an imperceptible shudder. Without knowing why, she wanted to run away, to escape from the spell that Nathan's eyes were exerting on her. The feeling intensified as Nathan continued, 'What interests me right now, though, is why *you're* here?' His rich voice was unexpectedly harsh.

And that was a good question to which she didn't have a good answer. She could hardly confess to the truth, which was, quite simply, that she had followed him unquestioningly, unthinkingly, as she might follow her fate. It was then that the full impact of Nathan's previous statement sank in. Her relationship with Matthew. What was that supposed to mean? He wasn't going to be difficult again, was he? Why *shouldn't* she have Matthew as a friend? She allowed her indignation to surface.

With a masterly shrug of indifference she settled for a half-truth.

'I didn't think,' she replied, a soft laugh of self-deprecation completing the picture of a woman who, although not sure of what was going on, didn't really care as she obviously felt in complete control. 'I just followed! But thank you very much for the wine.' She lifted her glass in a silent toast. 'Much appreciated after a long day.'

The throbbing muscle in Nathan's jaw showed itself again, and suddenly Rowan was grateful for the comforting presence of other staff, scattered around the room, singly and in small groups. Several of them she knew, even more she recognised by sight. She might have the impression that Nathan would gladly tear her limb from limb, but she was absolutely certain he wouldn't create a scene here. That knowledge emboldened her to ask, 'What was your second reason?'

Nathan looked confused by the question, and Rowan enlightened him. 'My relationship with Matthew is none of your business and I'm not prepared to discuss it. But you said there was something else. . .'

'Ah, yes.' Nathan's frown cleared and he reached inside his jacket to withdraw a letter. 'We might as well get this out of the way first. Pat's asked us to visit her, for tea, one day next week, and see how they've settled into their flat. We have to go.'

Of course they had to go; she didn't need to be told that. But there was no need for them to go together, and Rowan was quite sure Pat would rather have Nathan there alone. If that put him in a difficult position, too bad, she told herself. Why should she act as chaperon for him?

'I'm sure Pat would love to see you,' she confirmed, 'but you'd both be much happier without me to spoil your cosy tête-à-tête. You must be quite practised at dealing with your conquests now.'

Rather than annoying him, Rowan's snide comments acted to lighten Nathan's mood, and he actually smiled at her as he handed the letter across the table.

'Don't be bitchy. Pat's written a charming letter on behalf of her, Jean and Betty inviting you, me and Jenny to tea. We're going to go, and *you* are going to be gracious and professional about it.'

Knowing he was right only made Rowan feel worse, and she accepted the rebuke feeling very much like a naughty child who had been caught behaving badly.

'When are we going?' she asked without further comment.

'Jenny thought next Wednesday,' Nathan replied, outlining the plans and leaving Rowan feeling put out that he had discussed it with the OT first.

'Fine. I'll see her about details.' Rowan finished the last of her wine in one gulp, suddenly wanting to be gone.

'Good. That's settled.' Nathan's expression became grimmer. 'That brings us back to my main reason for wanting to talk to you.'

'I told you, I'm not discussing it.' Rowan moved, preparatory to leaving.

'Yes, you are.' The vehemence in his voice pinned her to her seat. 'You're at least going to hear me out. I'll make no pretence of saying I'm anything but disturbed by your relationship with Matthew. It's not only that you're years older than him, but I can't believe you really care about him. You wouldn't respond to me as you do if you had strong, serious feelings about another man. You enjoy flirting, Rowan, and that's fine. I know the rules of the game and I'm more than happy to play that game with you. But not Matthew.'

'You don't understand——' she began.

'You don't deny he was at your flat for dinner last night?'

'No.'

'And that it was very late when he got home?'

'No. But. . .' Slowly Rowan shook her head.

Matthew had got into the habit of having dinner with her once, sometimes twice a week, updating her on his studies, telling her tall stories of student pranks and making her laugh at the foibles of other members of the academic staff. They both enjoyed the evenings, and she saw no harm in them.

'He talks about you all the time. It's "Rowan this. . ." and "Rowan said that. . ."'

Rowan frowned at that, startled by what Nathan was telling her. It hadn't occurred to her that Matthew talked about her to his father—especially when he only mentioned Nathan indirectly to her. Somehow she had imagined her name was a taboo topic in the Pride household. Why would Matthew talk about her? Yet again she experienced the feeling that Matthew was in some way trying to control her life, but she still didn't understand to what purpose.

'I thought taking you out might have put him off you, but it doesn't seem to have done,' Nathan went on. 'I think it's quite irresponsible of you to have let this infatuation develop so far.'

The comment about taking her out stunned her. Not knowing whether to believe it or not, she was defenceless. She could only focus on the second half of what he had said. 'But he——'

Nathan cut across her denial. 'Maybe you're right. Maybe there isn't anything to discuss. I want you to leave Matthew alone—I've said it before and I'll go on saying it until you do. Will you?' Maybe if he hadn't sounded so belligerent, quite so impossibly arrogant, reflected Rowan later, she might have reacted differently. As it was, temper got the better of her, and her answer came out bald and defiant.

'No.'

Nathan paled slightly, causing Rowan to realise that he hadn't expected her defiance, that he had expected her ultimately to bow to his wishes. Swallowing hard, he braced himself, visibly steeling himself to ask the next question.

'The only thing I need to ask is, do you love him?'

Despite the clatter and the chatter of noise around

them from other people in the bar the silence between them stretched deep and endless.

When Rowan spoke her answer was the very opposite of what she had intended to say.

'Yes.'

And she did love Matthew, she admitted. He was kind and charming, clever, fun to be with, as affectionate as a young puppy, a whole host of things. But above all he was Nathan's son. How could she do anything but love him? She struggled to find the right words to qualify her answer to Nathan, but it was too late. She heard his intake of breath, but nothing else was said. While she was gathering her scattered wits Nathan had left the bar, left her alone once again at the mercy of her confused thoughts and doubts.

The flat was delightful. Jean's choice of colours had proved a great success, and it was bright and attractive and immaculately clean and tidy.

'I think Jean's developing obsessive tendencies,' Pat confided loudly to their guests. 'She makes us pick up and clean up all the time!' In the background Betty nodded vigorously.

Jean smiled demurely. 'Less of the cheek, young lady.' She addressed the remark to Pat with good humour, while Jenny and Rowan looked on open-mouthed and Nathan suppressed a smile.

As tea progressed, with daintily made sandwiches and cake, it became apparent that the oddly assorted threesome was working out well. Jean and Betty mothered Pat, who, to the delight of the staff members, appeared not only to enjoy it but to thrive on it. At the same time Pat was able to inject some life and sense of fun into the two older women, encouraging them to get out and about and try new things. Jean was the organiser of the 'family', but Betty had a role too, her stolid presence a welcome reassurance.

It was with something approaching triumph that the three emerged into the blustery autumn air, the visit having gone well, and all three women adjusting better than could have been hoped for.

'It's times like this it all seems worthwhile,' Jenny murmured to Rowan, but it was Nathan who replied.

'You have every right to feel a sense of pride in your accomplishments,' he told Jenny generously. 'Those women wouldn't be doing half so well without your dedication.'

Jenny blushed prettily under Nathan's benevolent regard, as they reached Jenny's car, with Rowan's parked neatly behind it, but there was no sign of Nathan's Volvo. As though reading her mind Nathan answered Rowan's unspoken question.

'Jenny brought me out here. Since she lives in the opposite direction I thought you could drop me off back at the hospital.' Smiling as he spoke, he made it sound as though it was the most natural thing in the world that she should give him a lift, as though they were close friends in the habit of doing small favours for each other.

For the second time that afternoon Rowan felt her mouth drop open, but she struggled to conceal it from Jenny, who obviously assumed there would be no problem in the arrangement.

Nathan's broad frame filled the passenger seat and threatened to overwhelm her, or at least that was the impression Rowan had. In reality she knew that it was his psychological impact as much as his physical presence that was crowding her, but that didn't help as she noisily crashed through gears starting the car. Nathan was a model passenger, not fussing or fretting; his hands didn't grip the dashboard or the side of his seat, but lay loosely in his lap, and, as far as she could tell, his foot wasn't moving to a phantom brake pedal with her every move. Just when she had decided he wasn't going to say anything until he was safely back with his car he surprised her by speaking, and astounded her by offering an apology.

'I'd like to apologise for my behaviour last week,' he announced formally. 'My only excuse is my concern for my son.'

'You have nothing to be concerned about,' Rowan told him, glad of the opportunity, she thought, to explain her strange answer in the affirmative.

'No, I think I realise that now. I don't believe you'd deliberately hurt Matthew. And age is no barrier to feelings. I should know that,' he added, somewhat cryptically.

'I don't think you understand. . .' Rowan tried to tell him, wondering how she was going to explain and at the same time trying to give most of her attention to the busy rush-hour traffic. It was with relief that she saw the hospital gates looming in the distance. Safely parked in the car park, they might be able to talk more sensibly.

'I don't want to discuss it further,' Nathan told her evenly but firmly. 'You were right to point out that it was none of my business.'

Rowan drew to an untidy halt by Nathan's car and turned to him, intent on making him listen to her. Nathan, however, had other ideas. Releasing his seat-belt, he opened the car door. Half out of the car, however, he seemed to have second thoughts, for he sat down again and turned back to her.

'If Matthew makes you happy, so be it — if that's what you want. But if I find that you're playing with him — then God help you!'

CHAPTER NINE

'ROWAN, have you seen Dad lately?' Matthew's question filled her with alarm, and she had the premonition that she was about to hear something she would much rather not. 'How did he seem to you?' Matthew wasn't meeting her eyes as he asked the question, which worried Rowan further.

'OK,' she admitted guardedly, totally at a loss to know what sort of answer Matthew expected. She didn't know if Nathan had said anything to his son regarding his concern over their relationship. She guessed he hadn't, in case it drove a wedge between them, whereas a wedge between Rowan and himself would be of no matter. Hadrian's Wall between them wouldn't matter.

She waited for Matthew to say something else, but nothing was forthcoming.

'Matthew?'

The slight twitch of his shoulders confirmed that Matthew had heard her but was deliberately remaining silent.

'Tell me,' she demanded, 'is Nathan all right? He's not ill, is he?'

Something in her voice must have got through to Matthew, for at last he turned to look at her, and she could see concern written in every line of his face. The lines of worry, rather than ageing him, only served to emphasise his youth, the softness of his features. Playful puppy eyes shouldn't know about such anxiety. Rowan waited in suspense for the worst to come, but in the end Matthew only shrugged. 'There's something wrong with him, but I don't know what.' With a shattering about-face he shrugged again. 'But let's forget Dad. What are we going to do tonight?'

Rowan was so astounded that she would have liked to shake him until his teeth rattled. How dared he worry her like that, and then say it was nothing? She was left thoroughly confused. Was there something wrong with Nathan or not?

Even for the end of November the afternoon was unusually dark and dreich. The yellow glow of the streetlamps, rather than shedding light, seemed to make the winter darkness more drear, and it was with a heavy heart that Rowan drove through the depressing streets of the housing estate.

As usual she was thinking about Nathan. They were still working on the genetics together, and had even had a couple of meetings to put some of the family trees in order. But though they met in the evenings it was always in Nathan's office, and he never suggested dinner, or even a drink. The most she was offered was a cup of coffee from the machine down the corridor. His manner was reserved, constrained, but they managed the work. Sometimes, as though he forgot to be on his guard, the Nathan who had so charmed her slipped through and she basked in his warm regard. But something always made him retreat into a coolly professional shell. Maybe Matthew was right, and there was something wrong with him.

It was with a supreme effort that Rowan dragged her attention away from Nathan and back to the other problem that was uppermost in her mind. At Jenny's request she had gone to visit Maggie and the other women sharing the second of the flats. Jenny was right;

it wasn't working. Maggie, although competent and able to care for herself and the flat, was getting on the nerves of the others. Her repetitive chanting had grown steadily worse, rather than improving as everybody had hoped it would when she was discharged. she was quite oblivious to the disruption and aggravation this caused the other women. And Dora had certainly gone downhill and looked as though she was becoming psychotic again.

Jenny had tried to set up a tea 'meeting' again, hoping that Nathan could make an informal assessment. The women, however, had other ideas and refused to extend an invitation. On the other hand, they hadn't refused Jenny and Rowan entry when they had turned up unexpectedly. They had agreed that something would have to be done before the whole situation became untenable. Not only did they want to prevent the women's problems getting worse, they wanted to prevent trouble with the neighbours. They knew that once neighbours started complaining the relationship between them all would deteriorate rapidly. Even if they patched things up it would never be the same again. There would always be the memory of the disruption, and neighbours would be looking for any excuse to complain again.

It had reluctantly been decided that Dora needed re-admission, and Rowan knew she had gone back into hospital that morning. It was thought that Maggie might do well living on her own, but that left the problem of finding somewhere for her. Decisions needed to be taken quickly, but it was difficult when there were only limited resources.

With all her ruminations Rowan realised she had taken the wrong turning somewhere and, rather than heading towards the motorway, she was heading deeper and deeper into the housing estate. Chastising herself for her loss of concentration, she tried to take stock of her bearings before admitting she was lost. Checking her rear-view mirror, she realised she was the only car actually moving in the gloomy landscape. Making an abrupt U-turn, she retreated the way she had come. As she turned into a road which, the second she had, she was convinced was the wrong way, a group of youths caught her attention. There seemed to be something awfully familiar about one of them. Slowly Rowan drove towards them, her curiosity overcoming her apprehension, just as they moved under a streetlamp.

Danny. No wonder he had looked familiar. The young man in the centre of a group of four youths was none other than her patient Danny MacNamara. She could just imagine what had happened. He had wandered off for a walk and, doing no harm to anybody, had more than likely been talking to himself. He would have been an easy target for the taunts of the other lads, although it now looked as though it had gone beyond that and was about to get violent. Rowan put her foot down and raced towards them, squealing to a halt as she reached them. A couple of the lads looked across at the car, possibly wondering if this was the cavalry come to the rescue. Seeing a lone woman, they obviously decided that it wasn't, and ignored her. It was only as she stepped out of the car that Rowan began wondering if this was the wisest thing to be doing. But it was too late to change her mind. Danny had seen her, and the look of hope that sprang into his eyes couldn't be denied. She had no choice but to go through with it. There was no time to go for help. That left praying for someone to come along.

'Leave him alone.' She spoke as authoritatively as

she knew how, but with the forlorn hope that they would do so. 'Danny, come with me.' She stretched out her hand to the terrified youth, her own heart beating wildly, and hoped against hope that it would all work out.

For a moment it looked as though it might. Danny started towards the safe protection of her outstretched hand, and the temerity of her actions had apparently shocked the others into momentary immobility. It was not to last. With a vehement curse one of the youths knocked her hand out of the way, starting a chain reaction as each of the others turned to look at her, placing themselves between her and Danny.

Their pronounced Glaswegian accents made much of what they said incomprehensible to her, for which she was grateful, as the little she could make sense of was not promising. The words most easily identifiable were obscenities, the rest apparently referred to what they intended to do with an interfering woman. Rowan tried to scream, hoping that someone in the deserted landscape would hear and take enough notice to phone the police, but no sound came from a parched throat constricted with fear.

A noise behind her caught her attention, but she dared not take her eyes off the lads in front of her to find out what was happening. If it was reinforcements she just prayed it was for the 'good guys' rather than the other side. Dimly she was aware of a car stopping and pounding feet. A voice called something, then again.

'Rowan!'

She was hallucinating. Who on earth could possibly be calling her name? She decided she was definitely hallucinating when she realised it sounded like Nathan.

As she was still trying to make sense of what she

thought she was hearing Nathan loomed into sight to stand beside her, at once dwarfing the youths and immediately making them less substantial, less threatening. Reckoning the odds, Rowan decided they weren't out of trouble yet. Their chances doubled as Mike Knight appeared as if by magic at her other side. Not for nothing had he been the star of the university's rugby team for the five years he had been there. Big at eighteen, he had filled out until now he was the size of a small bull. As he shook the hair out of his eyes Rowan could almost visualise him pawing the ground, preparatory to charging.

'I've phoned for the police, boss,' the giant announced clearly, causing the gang to cast quick looks at one another. One mumbled something that Rowan didn't understand but Mike apparently did. He added nonchalantly, looking at the youth, 'Carphone.'

Thank God for modern technology, was Rowan's only coherent thought as she felt her legs beginning to buckle. Now that it looked as though it was going to be all right the adrenalin which had kept her going acted to turn her to quivering jelly.

'Get in the car, Rowan,' Nathan instructed her curtly, but she was rooted to the spot, unable to move without assistance.

Whether her lack of action emboldened him, or whether it was something else, Rowan was later to ponder over, but without warning the leader of the group lunged towards her, grabbing at her and attempting to pull her towards him. A muffled roar came from somewhere deep in Nathan's throat, and Rowan was thrust roughly aside to safety as Nathan's right fist swung through the air, connecting with a satisfying crack on the youth's jaw. As though in slow motion the latter stopped before slowly and gracefully crumpling into an untidy heap. The three remaining youths took a step back, bringing them nearer Danny, whom they apparently had forgotten and only now recalled as their first objective. One of them went to catch hold of him just as Danny spotted a running figure in the distance.

'Iain! Iain!' He started to jump up and down, waving arms wildly above his head, the unexpected movement from the previously docile lad throwing his attacker off balance so that he collided with the other two. Rowan recognised with added relief that the figure pounding down the road towards them was indeed Danny's brother to his rescue.

Nathan and Mike moved close to the three youths now untangling themselves, the deep, guttural growls emitting from Mike as he bared his teeth enough to send the three further back, away from her, now also away from Danny. A familiar wailing sounded in the distance and was the final straw. The three youths took to their heels, running towards, and then around, Iain, but in the opposite direction to the approaching police car. With a mighty bellow Mike set off after them, hurling Gaelic curses as he went, but even Rowan could see he didn't really intend to catch them.

'It's all right, you're safe now — I've got you.' Iain was hugging his terrified brother, his soothing voice and actions calming Danny down now that he realised the danger was past.

Nathan put his arm around Rowan and pulled her to him. His touch broke the fear that had held her immobile and she collapsed against him, burying her face in his shoulder as she gasped for breath and strove for control. If she could only maintain her composure until she got home, then she could cry all she wanted. And she wanted to very much.

Dimly she was aware of Mike returning, and hauling the now semi-conscious gang leader to his feet, dangling him from his massive hand by the scruff of his neck while two police cars disgorged officers who immediately bundled him into the back of one of them.

Some part of her mind registered that Nathan, taking charge, was answering questions and issuing instructions. All she could do, all she wanted to do, was stay within the circle of his arms while he spoke over her head, calmly dealing with all the details, while his hand stroked her hair, letting her know he hadn't forgotten her need, but the loose ends needed clearing up.

One police car with a very subdued youth inside set off for the police station, the driver saying they would get details from Rowan later, and another officer volunteered to take Danny and Iain home. Nathan told them to go, that Mike would be along shortly to check Danny out. When they had gone Rowan felt more able to surface and face her rescuers.

Pushing her hair back from her eyes, she stepped out of the safety of Nathan's embrace and turned a woebegone face on the two men.

'Thank you.' The words were cracked, husky and very little more than a whisper, but came from the heart.

Nathan said nothing, but Mike grinned at her. 'Anything for a fair maiden in distress.'

The lighthearted words forced a wan smile to her lips, but the movement was her undoing. Her lower lip trembled ominously, while tears filled her eyes. With an almost incongruous gentleness Mike brushed the moisture from her lashes with his thumb.

'Don't cry, pretty lady,' he murmured. 'Remember how brave you were, confronting them.'

Wanting to tell him she hadn't felt brave at all, Rowan remained speechless, knowing that to try to say anything would be the signal for the tears to begin in earnest.

It was Nathan who saved her from the ignominy of breaking down. His words were brusque, abrupt but exactly what she wanted to hear. 'Come on, let's get you home.'

Blindly she turned towards her car, only to be caught and hauled back against the strength of Nathan's body.

'What do you think you're doing?' Nathan's voice rasped in her ear, while his very closeness made her conscious of the wild beat of his heart.

'Going home.' What else was there to say? To do?

'Don't be stupid, woman. You're in no state to drive.' He sounded so cross that instinctively Rowan tried to break away, but an encircling arm prevented movement, holding her tighter than ever. 'You're coming home with me.'

'But my car. . .' Rowan didn't understand why she was making a fuss. What she needed now, more than anything, was for Nathan to take care of her.

'Mike will go and see Danny, then drive it home for you.'

'But. . .'

'It will be my pleasure, fair damsel,' Mike confirmed with a broad wink. 'The keys. . .' he looked down at the car '. . .are still in the ignition.'

Nathan started to propel Rowan towards his car as Mike manoeuvred his bulk into the driving seat, when Rowan remembered something.

'The starter motor. . .' she turned back to Mike '. . .it's a bit temperamental, and. . .'

'And nothing he can't deal with,' Nathan insisted, not allowing her to stop moving, urging her into the warm safety of his car.

Her hands trembled and fumbled with the seatbelt until Nathan took it out of her hands and fastened it himself.

As they neared then passed the motorway turn-off which would have led to Rowan's part of the city she realised Nathan wasn't slowing the car, but was maintaining his speed.

'Where are we going?' she enquired with some bewilderment.

'Home,' came the terse reply. 'My home.' His voice sounded so strange that Rowan glanced at him anxiously, realising that she hadn't really looked at him since the unhappy incident had started. It was shocking to her to see the harsh, taut lines of his face, they grey cast to his skin, the rigidity with which he was holding himself. He looked the way she felt.

The welcoming warmth of Nathan's home surrounded her, but still she felt cold, holding herself tense as she suppressed the trembling that threatened to overtake her. Matthew darted into the hall, his face breaking into a broad grin as he saw who was there.

'Rowan! Lovely to see you. What are——?' He broke off abruptly as he took in her white face and now shaking limbs. 'What's wrong? Dad?' He saw his father just behind her, his face ashen, his body rigid. 'Dad! What's happened? Tell me!' He looked back to Rowan, taking her gently by the arm. 'Rowan——'

The human contact was her undoing. With a half-released sob Rowan flung herself at Matthew and was enveloped in his bear-hug as he gathered her close, his arms automatically closing round her to hold and comfort her.

A strangled gasp escaped Nathan, who muttered half under his breath, 'I need a drink,' and headed for the living-room.

Raising her head from the comforting curve of Matthew's neck, Rowan met Nathan's gaze.

'Nathan——' She didn't know what she was going to say, but didn't get a chance to finish it as Nathan's dark gaze raked her, his face anguished.

'God, Rowan, never, ever do that again. I was so scared when I saw you——' He fought for control, and suddenly Matthew's arms weren't enough, even as a substitute. She wanted to be comforted by Nathan, and she wanted to offer him comfort. She wasn't aware of moving, but without warning she was out of Matthew's embrace and falling headlong into Nathan's waiting arms.

As he gathered her to him, his strong arms tightening to press her body close to his, his head came down to rest against hers, his cheek rubbing against the top of her head in a gesture both giving and receiving reassurance and solace.

Her arms wound round him, holding him tightly as she buried her face in his chest as at long last the not-to-be-denied tears flowed freely. Flooding from her eyes, they were mopped up by Nathan's shirt-front as she sobbed and struggled for breath, while he held her and rocked her, soothing her with soft words of comfort while his strong hands consoled her. As the tears ebbed and her breathing eased she nestled into the curve of Nathan's arms, unwilling to leave their warmth, aware of the spreading damp patch on his shirt caused by her tears. She relaxed her hold on him and let one hand trail down from his shoulder until it rested lightly against the evidence of her outburst.

'I've made you wet,' she snuffled, choking back another sob. 'I'm sorry.'

His answer was to tighten his hold on her, then release her slightly, one hand gently raising her chin so that he could look into her face. 'I'll always be here for you to cry on,' he told her, his eyes inexplicably serious while his mouth curved to tell her a damp shirt was a small price to pay.

'Will someone tell me what's going on?' Matthew almost shouted the words, and Rowan started with guilty awareness that she had forgotten he was there.

With quiet authority Nathan ushered her into the living-room, trailed by Matthew, whose concern kept him darting around them while Nathan carefully installed Rowan on the sofa and then went to pour them a drink. He handed her a large brandy with the ghost of a smile. 'Drink that. You need it. I know I do.'

Rowan began to protest, but he pushed the glass into her hands. Sipping the fiery liquid, she had to admit that it was bringing back warmth and life to her numbed senses, but doing nothing for the pounding in her temples signalling the beginnings of a headache.

Nathan downed his drink in one swallow. 'God, I needed that!' He almost collapsed on the sofa next to her. 'Don't *ever* do that to me again.' He spoke harshly, but his eyes were concerned and he reached to squeeze her hand.

'Do *what*?' Matthew was looming over them, almost beside himself with curiosity, concern and anxiety. Rowan's guilt intensified as she acknowledged that they had virtually ignored him since they had arrived. But guilt didn't give her the emotional energy to talk to him. She fluttered her hands in his direction and looked beseechingly at Nathan, who succinctly informed Matthew what had happened.

'How could you be so stupid?' Matthew's anger was as unexpected as it was swift. 'Anything could have happened to you.'

'But it didn't.' Rowan quietly voiced the fact, while her fingers massaged her throbbing temples, trying to ease the pain.

Nathan noticed the gesture and shot a warning glance at Matthew, who either didn't see it or chose to ignore it.

'Suppose Dad hadn't come along——'

'But he did!'

'Matthew!' Rowan and Nathan spoke together, but Matthew took no notice.

'— what do you think would have happened?'

An involuntary gasp escaped Rowan's lips as she shuddered at what Matthew was trying to make her face — at what she was equally determinedly pushing away.

'That's enough!' Nathan's command slammed into Matthew with all the finesse of a sledge-hammer. 'Rowan doesn't need you making her feel worse. She knows——'

'I don't think——'

Rowan could stand the bickering no longer. The tears she had managed to master threatened to overwhelm her again, and with their moisture glittering on now wet, spiky lashes she turned on the two men.

'Stop it! Stop it, both of you. Maybe I didn't do the best thing, the most sensible thing — I don't know. All I know is Danny was in trouble and I couldn't leave him. Now let's just thank God that Nathan and Mike arrived when they did and forget it.'

'But——' Matthew was patently ill disposed to let go of the subject, but it was Nathan who again took charge.

'Forget it, Matthew.'

'But——'

'Now!'

Matthew was silenced, but Rowan could tell from his sulky look and thrust-forward lower lip that she hadn't heard the end of it. Matthew would come back to this topic with a vengeance; of that she had no doubt.

Sinking back into weary introspection, she was only dimly aware of Nathan and Matthew conversing softly together. It was the sound of the front door closing that jolted her back to awareness and the realisation that Nathan still had her hands clasped in his, his thumb slowly rubbing across the back of her hand in a lazy caress that was playing havoc with her heart-rate.

Without being obvious about it she tried to free her hands, and was disappointed when Nathan let go immediately. But it was only her hands he let go as his own went up to frame her face and he looked deep into her eyes. In the dark depths of his she could read the terror and anguish he had felt, was still feeling, on her account. His thumb traced the line of her jaw, his hand sliding to the back of her head, while her eyes remained mesmerised by his.

'Nathan...' His name was a whisper, dragged from her being, uttered without volition or meaning.

'Ah, Rowan...' he whispered back, as his head descended towards hers. 'What you do to me...' His hand firmly propelled her head forward to meet his.

Their lips met, and Rowan allowed herself to be pushed backwards as Nathan's weight eased them into a semi-lying position. Greedily she returned his kiss, her arms winding around him, unwilling, unable to think rationally while his body was pressed so close to hers. Enfolded in Nathan's arms she felt truly safe, protected, and she knew she wanted to stay like this forever.

Minutes merged into hours, or it could have been merely seconds passing into minutes—she had no notion of the time—when she remembered that there were still many unresolved issues between them, her relationship with Matthew not least of them. So well did their bodies come together that it was easy to overlook everything else, to forget that any problems existed.

A door banging in the distance penetrated her numbed mind and she heard Matthew calling, 'I'm back.'

Frantically she pushed at Nathan, instantly embarrassed, not wanting Matthew to come in and find them wrapped together in a close embrace as they lay full-length on the sofa. Nathan was in no hurry to let her go, reluctantly levering himself into a sitting position, his mouth a twisted grimace of wry self-deprecation.

'My apologies if I took advantage of your fragile state, but you're not going to try and tell me now that you love Matthew.' His voice was an odd mixture of anger and contempt, softened by what seemed to be genuine concern for her current condition and not a little confusion.

'No, of course not. Nathan, we have to talk——'

'Damn right we do!' The anger surfaced, but he made a visible effort to bank it down, judging her unable to deal with it yet.

A rattle at the door-handle announced Matthew's entrance, and he made a great play of letting them know he was coming in. It crossed Rowan's mind that he must have suspected something, but she didn't have the energy to think about the implications of that.

'Dinner is served,' he announced with a low bow and a flourish of the hand.

'What?' Food was the last thing on her mind, but the appetising smell wafting through was beginning to make her wonder if she hadn't been too hasty in dismissing the idea. It was by now the middle of the evening, and she had only managed time for a scrappy lunch.

'It seemed the easiest way to get us back to normal,' Nathan told her, while Matthew added,

'I've been out for an Indian. Come and eat it before it gets cold.'

'I'm not really hungry,' Rowan protested half-heartedly, but didn't resist when Nathan pulled her to her feet.

'Nonsense, woman.' He pulled her towards the door, his hold on her hand tight enough to let her know struggling was no use.

'Good heavens!' The loaded table brought the cry involuntarily to her lips, and even Nathan seemed taken aback by the abundance of steaming, aromatic containers.

'I don't know about you——' Matthew eyed the food appreciatively '—but worry makes me hungry. I'm starving!' He held out a chair for Rowan, who was led to it by Nathan, who only let go of her hand when she was seated, while Matthew poured them all wine.

Rowan maintained she wasn't hungry until she took her first mouthful of the delicately spiced, creamy chicken korma, when she instantly changed her mind and decided that she too was ravenously hungry. It was only as she allowed Matthew to ladle more of the lamb tikka on to her plate while she pulled off a piece of nan that she noticed Nathan was hardly eating. Matthew was making inroads into the food as only an eighteen-year-old male could, and she wasn't doing too badly herself, but Nathan was pushing the food round his plate rather than eating it, lines of tension etched on his face.

Nathan made coffee, and as they sat over it Rowan realised that he had been right. The cheerful meal had taken all her attention and she had, for a time, been able to forget the earlier events. Remembering still made her blood run cold, but already she was able to view the incident with greater detachment.

'I really should be going.' She stood up as she spoke, knowing that unless she made a determined effort it would be too easy for her to be talked into staying. A glance at her watch caused her to exclaim — she hadn't realised how late it had got. She was halfway to the hall before she realised she had no way of getting home, the knowledge bringing her to an abrupt halt, causing Nathan, who was hot on her heels, to bump into her.

'I don't have my car,' she told him plaintively, as though he didn't already know, and heard her voice wobble. She had been cocooned from thought and also from decisions for the past couple of hours, and the need to take control again was more than she could deal with.

'Dad can drive you home.' She heard Matthew volunteer his father jauntily and her heart missed a beat. She both wanted to be alone again with Nathan and at the same time wanted to postpone the inevitable discussion — at least until she was feeling stronger and had her thoughts marshalled in better order.

'No, I can't, I've had too much to drink,' Nathan announced harshly. 'And so have you,' he flung over his shoulder at Matthew before he could say anything else. 'I'll phone for a taxi.'

As always the taxi was perverse. When Rowan would have happily waited half an hour for one to come, it arrived within five minutes.

'What are you doing?' Matthew was helping her on with her coat when she noticed Nathan struggling into his sheepskin jacket.

'Taking you home,' he informed her shortly, as he met her eyes, holding them transfixed. 'You couldn't possibly imagine I'd put you in a taxi and send you home on your own?'

'There's no need.'

'Don't argue.' The two men spoke together, and Rowan gave in, not wanting to argue anyway.

The journey passed in silence and, caught in a welter of ambivalent emotions compounded by profound tiredness, Rowan could only be thankful. Somehow her hand had ended up in Nathan's comforting clasp again, and she didn't want anything more demanding from him at the moment. She had a second's unease when he got out of the taxi with her, but breathed more easily when she heard him instruct the driver to wait. He unlocked her door, then turned her to face him, his hands holding her lightly by the shoulders.

'I have to go to London to a meeting for a few days. I'll be back Sunday evening and then we're going to have a long-overdue talk.'

Nodding her agreement, Rowan could see that it would be useless to disagree. For a moment Nathan's grip tightened and he pulled her closer.

'I hate to leave you alone. Are you sure you'll be all right?'

She nodded again, but managed to find enough voice to reassure him, 'Yes, fine.' Much as she wanted to deny it, to ask him to stay, she knew she had to get over the hurdle of being on her own. And the sooner the better.

Nathan's arms slipped round her as he held her tightly to him for a moment, then dropped a light kiss on her waiting mouth before pushing her through the door.

'Till Sunday,' he murmured, and was gone.

CHAPTER TEN

'MATTHEW, I'm going to have to stop eating with you before I end up enormously fat.' Rowan pushed her plate away and leaned back in her chair, focusing on the word 'replete' as she dismissed the possibly more appropriate 'stuffed' as altogether too unladylike. 'You're turning into a very good cook,' she complimented him. 'You'll make some lucky girl a wonderful husband.'

'Yes, I will, won't I?' he agreed with tongue-in-cheek complacency.

All he got by way of reply was a lazy grin as Rowan couldn't summon up energy for more than that, watching him stack the dishes in the dishwasher with practised competency.

They settled companionably to watch a video, a light romantic comedy Matthew had chosen, and she appreciated his efforts to entertain her and stop her brooding on what had happened. Although Nathan was away she didn't feel uncomfortable in his house this time, sure that he wouldn't object to her being there. His last kiss, gentle as it had been, had promised so much. On Sunday everything would be sorted out.

'Is that the time?' Rowan's glance focused on her watch almost uncomprehendingly. 'It can't possibly be one o'clock!'

'Time flies when you're having fun,' Matthew pointed out, and Rowan subsided with a responding grin. It was Friday night and not as though she had to be up early for work. Nevertheless it was time to go.

It had been a fraught week one way and another, and she needed her sleep. She wanted to be in shape to meet Nathan on Sunday.

Matthew stood by Rowan's car as she settled herself in, muttering, 'I don't like you going off on your own like this. I should really see you home.'

'Don't be silly. I'll be fine,' she assured him.

'Dad wouldn't just let you go off like this.'

Indeed he wouldn't, and that gave her a wonderfully combined *frisson* of pleasure together with a comfortable sense of contented complacency.

She turned the key in the ignition, and there was a muffled groan, dying away to silence. She tried again, and this time there wasn't even a groan. A few minutes later they decided the car was, if not dead, at least in a coma, and would require resuscitation and, more than likely, spare-part surgery.

'It's been playing up all week; I should have got something done about it before now,' Rowan sighed.

'Don't worry — you can stay here. The spare bed's made up.'

'I'll get a taxi.' Rowan was tempted to give in. It would be easy not to have to bother, but something inside her insisted it would be better if she went home — that Nathan wouldn't like her to stay.

When Matthew saw she was serious he phoned the taxi firm, coming back a few minutes later doing his best to look suitably sorrowful.

'They say it'll be at least an hour before a taxi can get here,' he told her, the smile he was trying so hard to suppress breaking through. 'There's no point in getting the AA out in the middle of the night, so you might as well stay.'

* * *

'I feel awful, sleeping so late.' Rowan didn't sound particularly contrite, sitting in the kitchen wrapped in the cosy blue towelling of Matthew's robe with the remains of a large breakfast strewn over the pine table.

'You must have needed it.' Matthew poured them both more coffee. 'Anyway, neither of us has to be anywhere, and I never get up early on Saturdays if I can help it.' He leant back in his chair, stretching his arms out to the sides, his robe gaping open to expose his bare chest as he yawned loudly. 'Sorry.'

A loud bang shattered the peace, and Matthew was struggling to his feet when the kitchen door burst open and Nathan erupted through it, his face dark with anger, his eyes shooting from Matthew to Rowan as he took in the state of their undress and the cosy domestic scene.

'What the hell's going on here?' he demanded, looking straight at Rowan, his eyes raking her from the top of her dishevelled head to her bare legs, her feet loosely clad in Matthew's too large slippers.

The sight of him unnerved her, and she drew herself upright in the chair, her hands automatically tightening the belt of the robe. The movement caused Nathan to look even more angry, and Rowan felt that he had stripped the fabric away, leaving her nakedly exposed to his critical gaze.

'Dad, what are you doing back so early?' Matthew was asking at the same time as Nathan, speaking before he took in his father's expression and realised that all was not well.

Nathan continued to stare at Rowan, and slowly it dawned on Matthew that his father was blazingly angry. His tentative, 'Dad?' was ignored.

'I'm waiting for an answer.' Nathan's gaze continued to bore into her. Rowan began to see the scene through his eyes and accepted how easily it could be misconstrued. The idea amused her, as she was sure it would amuse Nathan when it was all sorted out, causing a small, secretive smile to curve her lips.

'I'm glad you think it's funny,' Nathan snarled. 'I hope you still do by the time I've finished with you. For now, I want you out of my house.'

'Dad, you don't——' His father's interpretation was gradually filtering through to Matthew. Like Rowan, he found it amusing, and he too smiled.

It was a smile which seemed to be the final straw for Nathan. Grabbing Rowan by the arm, he hauled her to her feet.

'Out. Now. Take your scheming, seductive ploys out of my house and *leave my son alone*!'

As the full enormity of what his father was implying penetrated Matthew's resistant mind he saw red and lunged for his father, knocking him away from Rowan. There was a muffled curse from Nathan as the two men came together in an undignified scramble of bodies and fists. Before she could really see what was happening, or do anything to stop them, Nathan had Matthew pinned against the wall, holding him there with apparent ease, although they were both breathing heavily.

Shaking his son, Nathan breathed fire at him as he enunciated clearly, 'Forget her. She's not worth it, nothing more than a cheap tramp. She's only playing with you.'

'Nathan, listen——' She tried to make him listen to her, but it was as though she hadn't spoken, so effectively did he ignore her.

'Believe me, I know what she's really like. She's been trying her tricks on me. . .'

As the litany went on Rowan shut her mind to it and

rushed from the room. Throwing her clothes on, she regained some composure and tried to believe that when she went downstairs again it would be all sorted out and Matthew would have got his father to listen to him. She could hear raised voices and then the slamming of doors as she sat on the edge of the bed trying to plan what to say, which was where Matthew found her.

'You OK?' he asked, and when she nodded he continued, 'Come on, I'll take you home.'

'Nathan. . .?' she queried.

'Isn't here.' The total lack of emotion in his voice and impassivity of expression told Rowan that Matthew hadn't forgiven his father for what he had said, or thought. It didn't occur to her that Nathan hadn't listened to Matthew's explanation and denial until he told her.

'So the upshot is,' he concluded, 'Dad thinks we're having a torrid affair; that you seduced me and are now trying the same tactics on him.'

Hot colour coursed through her, leaving her cheeks scarlet as she realised that Nathan had left nothing out in trying to convince his son to his view of her.

'Nothing I said made any difference. He wasn't listening to half of it anyway.' Matthew's voice cracked, and it was then that Rowan understood that his control hid not disappointment, or regret, but blazing anger — a red-hot anger directed squarely at his father. 'I'll drive you home and then get your car seen to.'

'Didn't that convince——?'

'No!'

There didn't seem to be anything left to say, so Rowan silently followed Matthew to his car.

'Maybe he'll have calmed down by the time you get

back,' she said. 'Be more reasonable.' They were standing outside her flat.

Matthew shrugged. 'I don't care what he's like. He has no right to treat you like that. Or me.'

'He was upset. And concerned for you. . .' Rowan wondered why even now she was defending him. Nathan had behaved appallingly, jumping to quite unwarranted conclusions, yet she couldn't bring herself to hate him.

Matthew made a sound of disgust. 'That's not concern, that's——' He broke off. 'I'm moving out.'

'What? You can't.'

'I'll go back and get my stuff. One of the guys has been on at me to move into their flat. I'll go there.'

'Matthew, don't do anything rash. Your father——'

'My father can go to the devil for all I care! To think I tried. . . You're too good for him, Rowan.' With a quick kiss on her cheek Matthew had gone.

The ringing of the phone penetrated the dull fog that enveloped her. As she groped her way to it Rowan noted that it was getting dark and she had lost the day between bouts of introspective despair and fits of crying.

'Let me speak to Matthew.' The voice was unmistakable.

'He isn't here. Nathan——'

'Where is he?'

'Nathan, I——'

'His clothes have gone. Where is he?'

'He's gone to friends. I don't know——'

The tone sounding in her ear told her Nathan had hung up on her.

* * *

Matthew refused to speak to his father and Nathan refused to speak to her. She heard reports of his short temper, long hours of work, his haggard look, the demands he made of others and his willingness to be on call over Christmas. She bumped into Mike, who confided that he was worried about his boss, that he seemed determined to work himself to a standstill — and take his senior registrar with him.

'The amount of work he's getting through, he can hardly be sleeping,' he told Rowan morosely, 'and he expects me to keep up with him.'

Matthew refused to go back to his father's for Christmas and went off to stay with friends, washing his hands of both his parents.

Rowan moped through a family Christmas at her brother's and made an excuse to return home early. She couldn't help thinking of Nathan on his own, spending a lonely Christmas. The idea that he wasn't alone, but one of his glamorous girlfriends was with him, was even worse.

Matthew was also back early from his holiday, and Rowan tried to persuade him to see his father, knowing how much Matthew was missing him, even though he wouldn't admit it.

'It's nearly the New Year, Matthew. You can't start a brand new year not speaking to your father.'

'Watch me!' he retorted.

'That's just being childish.'

'He's the one being childish. He won't listen to me——'

'Maybe he will now,' urged Rowan. 'He's tried to contact you and you've cut him dead. He might be prepared to listen. Maybe it's up to you to be the mature one and contact him.' She did her best to appeal to Matthew's need to be grown up, to best his father, if it was a way of getting them back together. 'One of you has to start behaving like an adult rather than a spoilt brat. Why not you?'

She could see Matthew mulling over the idea, that it flattered him to think he could behave more maturely than his father.

'I could have a go at it, I suppose.' A frown tugged his eyebrows together as he gave the idea an inordinate amount of thought. Was it possible to have one last try at getting his father together with Rowan? He was convinced Nathan cared for her, but did he deserve her? It was stubborn pride which was preventing him doing anything about it. Hadn't he long ago said he wouldn't remarry, and frequently reiterated the shallowness of women? Matthew thought of his mother and accepted this as a description of her — but surely his father could see how different Rowan was?

'I've sort of made my peace with Dad,' Matthew told her on the phone.

'What does "sort of" mean?' Rowan queried.

'We've agreed to a truce and we're not mentioning you at all.'

'You mean he still believes——'

'It isn't the right time to try and convince him, believe me,' said Matthew. 'I'll try and get through to him soon, though. At the moment it takes us all our time to maintain a polite distance. But it's not me he's really angry at, it's you.'

'Well, as long as you're getting along together.' She tried to be pleased for them, but had to own that it was difficult not to feel abandoned.

New Year's Eve was a bad time to feel neglected and rejected, she thought as she mooned round the house, not settling to anything. There was a party she could go to, but she had already decided she couldn't face it. It would only emphasise how empty she felt. She would be better off staying in, going to bed early and ignoring the special significance of the day. What was another day, more or less?

'Rowan can you come over right away?' Matthew's voice was high-pitched and anxious, the words jerking out of him between gasps for breath.

'What's happened?' A cold fear clutched her heart as she waited for his explanation.

'It's Dad.'

Her heart turned over as it felt as though it was caught in a vice like grip. 'What's wrong? Is he all right?' Now it was racing at twice its normal speed and seemed to have lodged somewhere in her throat.

'Just get over here.'

The phone went dead.

Matthew must have been keeping a look-out for her, because as she hurried up the path towards the house he opened the door to her. Rushing inside, she was already asking questions.

'Where is he? What's happened?'

Matthew flapped his hands, shushing her, and she subsided into puzzled silence, moving further into the hall.

'Won't be a minute,' Matthew whispered, almost rudely pushing past her. Without warning he was through the door and closing it after him, and to her total bewilderment Rowan heard him turn the key in the lock. Vainly she turned the handle, but nothing happened. Matthew had locked her in. A rattle at the letter-box indicated that he was still there, and an envelope fluttered through. With complete incomprehension she bent to pick it up, reading the one word written on it—'DAD'.

While the one word sank in a feeling of utter dread stole over her as she began to have the glimmerings of what Matthew was doing—had done. Lifting the flap of the letter-box, she whispered fiercely, 'Matthew!' but knew it was too late as she heard his car start up.

For reasons best known to himself Matthew had locked her in the house. The enormity of it sank in. Presumably with his father.

I'll kill you, Matthew Pride, she thought vehemently, as she turned the letter over in her fingers. Slowly, painfully. I'll make you suffer. You'll be sorry. . . But ranting against Matthew wasn't getting her anywhere.

As she saw it, she could cower in the hall until Nathan came out and found her, or she could go looking for him. Neither choice was particularly attractive, but all things considered she decided she'd rather go looking for Nathan than be found cowardly loitering in the hall, afraid to face him. At least she would have the advantage of a surprise attack.

It was with trepidation that she pushed open the living-room door. The lamps were lit, there was a fire burning in the grate, soft music came from hidden speakers and she could see the top of Nathan's head as he sat with his back to the door.

Her mouth was parched as she struggled for words which would not articulate themselves. A half-strangled sound escaped her which caught Nathan's attention, but he did not turn round. 'Matthew?' he queried.

Rowan took a step further into the room, swallowing hard, praying for her voice to return. Something must have alerted Nathan that all was not right, for he swung round in his chair.

'Matth——' The word was cut short as he exploded, 'You!' leaping to his feet.

'Er — yes.' Luckily her vocal cords had come back to life.

'What the hell are you doing here?' Despite the dimness of the room Rowan could see that Nathan had lost colour and appeared to be having trouble speaking too as the words sounded as though they were being dragged out of him. That gave her a sense of increased confidence, so she sounded more in control as she replied.

'I'm not at all sure. Maybe this letter from Matthew will explain.'

'Letter? What letter? What the hell's going on?' With his voice and colour getting more heated with every word, it was as though as she watched him her own control grew stronger.

'Don't yell at me, Nathan Pride. It was your son who dragged me over here on a wild-goose chase.'

The mention of Matthew sent the colour flying from his face again as he turned positively ashen.

'Where's Matthew?' He looked over her shoulder as though by will-power he could make his son appear.

'I've no idea.' Rowan moved closer, the letter in her outstretched hand. 'I suggest you read this and then maybe we can piece together what's going on.'

'Hmm.' Nathan sounded less than convinced as he took the envelope from her, being careful their fingers didn't touch. Ripping it open, he took out a couple of sheets of paper and, to Rowan's surprise, another envelope. What was Matthew playing at?

For a moment Nathan looked so furiously angry that Rowan thought he was going to explode, but as he stared longer at the letter a strange calm seemed to steal over him and he faced her with a quirked eyebrow and a surprising lack of aggression.

'Apparently Matthew has locked us in and intends us to stay until we've sorted out our differences.'

'The back door——' Rowan twisted towards the door, driven by a panic she didn't understand not to be left alone with Nathan.

'You can try it if you like, but he's thorough. He says he's taken the keys to the windows as well!'

Her knees buckling under her without warning, Rowan subsided on to the arm of an armchair, totally devoid of sensible thought. She couldn't understand what Matthew was hoping to achieve by this prank, apart from further infuriating his father.

Not that Nathan looked particularly infuriated. It worried Rowan even more that although he looked decidedly wary there was something about him that indicated satisfaction. As she watched him carefully refold the letter and return it to the envelope she remembered the second one.

'What's the other envelope?' she asked.

She saw Nathan hesitate, tapping the letter against his hand as though deciding what to tell her. Eventually it seemed that only the truth would do as he held it towards her.

'It's addressed to you.'

Rowan turned her back on him to read it, not at all sure that she would be able to control her face, whatever it said.

Dear Rowan,
    I couldn't quite manage to gift-wrap Dad for you for Christmas. This is the best I could do. Make the most of the opportunity.

See you in the morning.
Love, Matthew

What did he mean? It couldn't possibly mean what she wanted it to mean, could it? Did Matthew guess how she felt about his father? Was he endorsing it? Did he expect them to get together? And if so, what did that imply about what he knew of Nathan's feelings?

'Does it say anything interesting?' Nathan sounded nonchalant, feigning uninterest while Rowan was struggling to reply.

'No.'

'Does he say when he'll be back?'

'Er — he implies not until the morning,' she admitted.

'Let me see.'

'No!' Fumbling fingers rammed it back into the envelope which she then thrust into her bag. It would be disastrous if Nathan got to see it.

She couldn't understand why her actions appeared to please Nathan, but she was sure they did.

'Since it looks as though we've the night to get through we might as well be civilised about it. Would you like a drink?' Acting the urbane host, Nathan sounded in complete control. He wasn't reacting as Rowan would have expected him to, and that filled her with a sense of deep foreboding.

Nothing explained Nathan's reaction. Ever since he had read Matthew's letter he had been acting oddly, almost as though he was waiting for something more to happen. But what?

Nervously twisting her glass between her fingers, Rowan decided that she might as well get it over with. If she and Nathan were going to row she would rather it was sooner than later. If it got too bad she would break a window and make her escape that way. She didn't intend to spend the night in these strange conditions, nor did she intend to miss this opportunity of speaking her mind to Nathan. A heartfelt sigh escaped her lips, and that was Nathan's cue to break the silence.

'Rowan?' His beautiful voice had a tenderness she couldn't remember hearing before and which disconcerted her. Was there any chance he had set this up with Matthew? No. His surprise and anger when he first saw her had been genuine enough.

Looking up from her contemplation of the drink she hadn't wanted and meeting Nathan's eyes, she changed her mind and decided some Dutch courage might not come amiss. A hasty gulp of the spirit caused her to splutter as its fiery strength hit the back of her throat and tears sprang into her eyes.

'Careful now,' Nathan advised, taking the glass from her and putting it down on the coffee-table. Recovering herself, Rowan forced her eyes to meet his.

'Nathan——' The melting brownness of his eyes mesmerised her so that she forgot what she had been going to say.

'Rowan.' The word was a caress.

'Nathan——' How to start? She wanted to clear the air, but there was so much to say.

'Rowan.' He was teasing her, his eyes laughing as he repeated her name.

'Nathan, we have to talk.' The words rushed out before she could lose her nerve totally.

'We've apparently got all night,' he affirmed, although she detected a slight change in his tone.

'Be serious.' The words snapped out, indicating how on edge she really was. 'There are things we need to clear up.' She detected a slight change in his posture at that, but was determined to continue. 'About Matthew——'

'You're not having an affair. You've never seduced him. I'm an arrogant fool. Yes, I know.'

'How. . .? When did Matthew tell you?' And why didn't he tell me? she thought.

'He didn't. But I now realise I was wrong in believing that of you.'

'So you've just decided, after all this time, to believe us?'

'Yes.'

'Why?'

'Because I realised that it's true and that I've been blind and more than a little prejudiced, which I want to explain. You've made me revise my opinion on a number of issues, Rowan,' Nathan told her.

Irrationally, rather than being pleased and relieved, Rowan was furiously angry. How dared he suddenly announce that he believed them after all, as though by so doing he excused everything he had done and said?

'And that's supposed to make everything all right, is it?' she snapped at him sarcastically.

'I hope it will if I apologise abjectly enough. And I do.' He sounded sincere, but not as sorry as Rowan wanted him to. He had put her through weeks of misery, and she wanted him to pay for that, to suffer as she had. He obviously expected her to be overwhelmed that he had deigned to apologise at all.

'Rowan?'

She detected a slight chink in his arrogance, a hint of uncertainty in how he said her name. Calling on all her acting skills, she looked straight at him. 'Apology accepted, Nathan.' She spoke coolly, offhandedly, as though his apology was of no consequence. 'Well, that finishes that topic of conversation, and I doubt if we have anything else to say to each other.'

Nathan looked absolutely stunned. It took all Rowan's self-control not to smile openly. She was right — he had expected her to fall at his feet in gratitude that the great Nathan Pride finally believed her.

'You don't sound as though you've really forgiven me,' he ventured, a smile playing around his lips as Rowan strenuously resisted being charmed by him.

'You're forgiven, Nathan,' she told him crisply. 'Don't expect me to keep repeating it.'

'You still sound bitter.' He proffered the opinion slowly. 'Can't you forget——?'

Something snapped at that and she raced into speech, interrupting him. 'Yes, I am bitter, and no, I can't just forget. Why shouldn't I be bitter? You've accused me of terrible things. . . you didn't believe a word I said. . .' Her voice was rising on a note of high-pitched hysteria as she gave way to her feelings, allowing the words to run away with her. 'How dare you just say you're sorry and expect everything to be forgiven and forgotten? You don't know what I've been through these past weeks——' Her voice wobbled out of control as the tears started to fall.

'Yes, I do.' Suddenly Nathan was out of his chair and sitting on the broad arm of hers, his hands drawing her close to him as he wrapped his arm round her while she gave way to noisy tears.

'There, there, my love,' he soothed. 'I know just how you've felt, but it's over now.'

'Leave me alone!' Rowan struggled half-heartedly in his embrace, but Nathan wisely ignored her, lifting her up so he could sink into the chair, drawing her down on to his lap.

'But don't you know *why* I was so angry, why I behaved as I did?' he asked gently.

'Because you're an arrogant pig!' She tried to sound severe, but with his hands roaming over her it wasn't easy. Her tears were fast disappearing as she snuggled into the warm safety of his arms, taking comfort from the strength with which he held her. Although she couldn't see his face, hers being buried in his chest, she knew he smiled. She could hear it in his voice.

'Yes, I'll admit that. But I was also jealous. Madly, insanely jealous of my own son.' His voice broke on the words. 'Can you imagine what that was like, Rowan?' His arms tightened round her as she tried to imagine what it had been like for a man as proud as Nathan to feel jealousy over his son.

'There was no need. I——'

'I know that now. But then. . . I was attracted to you from the first, and I thought you were attracted to me. Then the next thing I know you've employed Matthew. . . you were so close. . . had such an understanding. . . if it had been anyone else I would have dealt with it. They wouldn't have stood a chance. But Matthew. . .' He shuddered. 'How could I compete with my own son?'

'But you did. You kissed me and——'

'One of my better moves,' he retorted, and she could hear the confidence returning in his voice, as he tipped her head back and found her lips with his. It was as though a thousand flames flared into life, their heat and brightness coursing through her, and she gave herself up to him, twisting in his embrace so that she could more easily wind her arms round him. It was some time before either of them gave thought to further conversation, but it was Nathan who eased her away from him.

'Rowan, let me explain while I still have some coherent thought.'

'Mmm.' She nuzzled his neck, less interested now in any explanation than continuing her exploration of his body, sure that they could sort everything out, that it would all be understood.

But it seemed Nathan wanted her to understand now. 'I felt so old,' he murmured, his words causing Rowan to move away from him slightly so that she could pay more attention.

'You're not old, Nathan! I never thought. . .'

He gripped her hands more tightly. 'Compared to Matthew I am. And I'm ten years older than you. Watching the two of you together I felt as though I'd been put out to grass. That you saw me as Matthew's father, that you'd only see me as a father.'

'Nathan, you're being stupid. How could I possibly think of you as old?' She ran her fingers up his chest, her thumbs caressing his jaw. 'Especially after I'd seen you in those shorts.' She laughed, and was delighted to see Nathan look embarrassed.

'It's a long story, but Matthew set that up too. He knew you'd be coming over and——'

She silenced him with a swift kiss. 'I'm glad he did. I'd never have got to see your legs otherwise!'

'What does that mean?' Nathan sounded decidedly wary.

'They're well worth seeing!'

'It could be arranged again. Soon!' he told her meaningfully, laughing softly when it was her turn to blush.

'You kissed me and then ignored me. After Mull. . .' That still hurt, and she wanted an explanation.

'Everything was perfect there. I forgot about

Matthew. Then we came back and there he was, with you every day, talking about you. I thought you wanted him. After you'd kissed me I thought, hoped, you'd realise you made a mistake with Matthew, but you seemed even more determined to continue your relationship with him.' He held her tight, rubbing his head against her cheek. 'There were times when I wanted to destroy you both.' It was his turn to sound bitter, and Rowan was shocked.

'Nathan!'

'I love my son very much,' he informed her quietly, 'and I thought he was sleeping with the woman I was falling in love with. That's a very special kind of hell, Rowan. But you need to understand something of my marriage to really appreciate how I felt. I know Matthew has told you some of it, but what he probably doesn't know is that when my wife left me it was to go off with a man considerably younger than her.'

'Oh, Nathan, no!' So much of his anger was now made clear. It was a resentment against his wife more than her, and it also explained why he was so convinced that a relationship between her and Matthew was possible, despite the difference in their ages.

'It was as though it was all happening again. I tried to leave you alone, but I couldn't. Nor could I believe you really loved him, not when you responded to me. But you always backed away from me. Back to Matthew.'

'Because you seemed so willing to let go. You didn't try to hold me! I thought you were playing with me, that you'd wanted to find out something about me, and having done so you'd got bored. Your manner was so inconsistent, I didn't know where I stood.' Rowan shook her head at him. 'I love Matthew too,' she told him, even now feeling him tense as she said the words, 'but more as a younger brother than anything else. It's——' She stopped, aware that she had been going to confess her love for Nathan. But was that what he wanted? She still didn't know, and he had said nothing about loving her now.

As though understanding her uncertainty Nathan kissed her again.

'I love you very much, Rowan Stewart, and I devoutly hope that you love me.'

'Oh, yes, Nathan, yes.' She fell forward again into his waiting arms as he pressed her body to his, his hands splaying out across her back to hold her closely to him as further explanation waited while they continued their exploration of each other with questing hands and mouths.

His mouth travelling along her jawbone, Rowan felt his warm breath fan her ear, sending such waves of desire through her that she only half paid attention to what he was saying.

'You are going to marry me, aren't you?' he muttered, as his teeth nibbled at her earlobe.

'Mmm, yes,' she moaned, although she was more intent on his mouth on her than on either of their words.

She heard a grunt of satisfaction as his lips closed over hers again, and it was several minutes later when the full import of the exchange sank into her fevered brain.

'Nathan, did you just——?'

'Yes, and you accepted. You can't back out now.' His words were teasing, but his voice was completely serious.

'I wouldn't want to,' she advised him, basking in the love shining in his eyes. Then, recalling a puzzle, she asked, 'Why did you suddenly decide to believe there was nothing between Matthew and me?'

Nathan's eyes clouded over for a second, then cleared as he refocused on her. 'It wasn't that sudden. I think I've known for a while now that I've been punishing you for what my ex-wife did. I was ashamed of that, and somehow it made it even harder to approach you and say I was wrong. Stubborn pride, I suppose.' A wry smile twisted his lips. 'And then it was a good excuse for doing nothing. I was scared, you see, that even if you didn't love Matthew you still wouldn't want me.'

That seemed to call for reassurance, so Rowan hugged him more tightly, murmuring under her breath, 'Now that was silly.'

'When I read Matthew's note saying he'd locked us in I was so angry for a minute I didn't understand what he was doing. But then I read the rest of it and accepted what he was doing, and probably has been doing for months. He wants to get us together, and I can now see that he's been doing a lot to achieve it, even though it didn't always look like it. He was never going to let me forget you, that's for sure.'

'Yes.' With hindsight much of Matthew's behaviour took on a different meaning.

Nathan relaxed back in the deep armchair, taking her with him. 'And then he said that you were my Christmas present!' He grinned at Rowan, waiting.

'You're mine,' she confirmed.

'Cheeky young. . .' He laughed. 'I've just remembered something else he said earlier today—that I took my name too literally. I was letting pride stand in the way of what I really wanted. He even said, "I could give you what you really want but, knowing you, you'd be too proud to take it! Remember, pride comes before a fall!"' His smile faded as he found her mouth once more, murmuring against it, 'I don't know if that's what you are, my love, the downfall of my pride, but you're the only one I've fallen for, so you are, rightly, Pride's fall!'

As they settled to enjoy the rest of their night of enforced intimacy Matthew was explaining to Robbie how clever he'd been, after he'd turned up begging a bed for the night.

'Although they should have guessed,' he told his godfather almost despairingly. 'Why else would I take a woman's job?'

Mills & Boon

MEDICAL ROMANCE

The books for enjoyment this month are:

THE CONSTANT HEART Judith Ansell
JOEL'S WAY Abigail Gordon
PRIDE'S FALL Flora Sinclair
ONLY THE LONELY Judith Worthy

♥ ♥ ♥ ♥ ♥

Treats in store!

Watch next month for the following absorbing stories:

A BORDER PRACTICE Drusilla Douglas
A SONG FOR DR ROSE Margaret Holt
THE LAST EDEN Marion Lennox
HANDFUL OF DREAMS Margaret O'Neill

Available from Boots, Martins, John Menzies, W.H. Smith, most supermarkets and other paperback stockists.

Also available from Mills & Boon Reader Service, Freepost, P.O. Box 236, Thornton Road, Croydon, Surrey CR9 9EL.

Readers in South Africa - write to:
Book Services International Ltd, P.O. Box 41654, Craighall, Transvaal 2024.

PENNY JORDAN

A COLLECTION
Volume 2

From the bestselling author of *Power Play*, *The Hidden Years* and *Lingering Shadows* comes a second collection of three sensuous love stories, beautifully presented in one special volume.

Featuring:

FIRE WITH FIRE
CAPABLE OF FEELING
SUBSTITUTE LOVER

Available from May 1993   Priced: £4.99

W🌐RLDWIDE

Available from Boots, Martins, John Menzies, W.H. Smith, most supermarkets and other paperback stockists.
Also available from Mills & Boon Reader Service, Freepost, P.O. Box 236, Thornton Road, Croydon, Surrey CR9 9EL
(UK Postage & Packing Free)

Another Face...
Another Identity...
Another Chance...

When her teenage love turns to hate, Geraldine Frances vows to even the score. After arranging her own "death", she embarks on a dramatic transformation emerging as *Silver*, a hauntingly beautiful and mysterious woman few men would be able to resist.

With a new face and a new identity, she is now ready to destroy the man responsible for her tragic past.

Silver – a life ruled by one all-consuming passion, is Penny Jordan at her very best.

The international bestseller from the author of *Power Play* and *The Hidden Years*.

W RLDWIDE

Available from W.H. Smith, John Menzies, Martins, Forbuoys, most supermarkets and other paperback stockists.

Also available from Mills and Boon Reader Service, Freepost, P.O. Box 236, Thornton Road, Croydon, Surrey CR9 9EL

£3.99